The Ponytail Girls

What's Up With Her?

LEGACY PRESS

Other books in the Ponytail Girls series:

Book 1

Meet the Ponytail Girls

Book 2

The Impossible Christmas Present

Book 3

Lost on Monster Mountain

Book 4

A Stormy Spring

Book 5

Escape From Camp Porcupine

The Ponytail Girls

What's Up With Her?

Bonnie Compton Hanson

Dedication

To Ponytail Girls readers everywhere, and to the
wonderful women God can help you become.

THE PONYTAIL GIRLS/BOOK 6: WHAT'S UP WITH HER?
©2009 by Legacy Press, third printing
ISBN 10: 1-58411-084-8
ISBN 13: 978-1-58411-084-2
Legacy reorder# LP48046
JUVENILE FICTION / Religious / Christian

Legacy Press
P.O. Box 261129
San Diego, CA 92196

Cover illustrator: Terry Julien
Interior illustrator: Aline Heiser

Scriptures are from the *Holy Bible: New International Version* (North
American Edition), ©1973, 1978, 1984 by the International Bible Society.
Used by permission of Zondervan Bible Publishers.

Printed in the United States of America

Contents

~ Introduction ~

Welcome to the Ponytail Girls! Whether you wear a ponytail or not you can share in the adventures of Sam Pearson and her friends, the PTs (that's short for Ponytails). Just like you, the PTs love sports and shopping and fun with their friends at school.

The PTs also want to live in a way that is pleasing to God. So when they have problems and conflicts, they look to God and His Word, the Bible. They might also seek help from their parents, their pastor or their Sunday school class teacher, just as you do.

Each chapter in this book presents a new problem for your PTs to solve. Then there is a Bible story to help explain the Christian value that the PTs learned. A Bible memory verse is included for you to practice and share.

There may be words in this book that are new to you, especially some Bible names and Spanish words. Look them up in the Glossary on page 181, then use the syllables to sound out the words.

In addition to the stories, in each chapter you will find questions to answer and fun quizzes, puzzles, and other activities. Also, at the end of each chapter starting with Chapter 1, you will get a clue that leads to finishing the Winner's Circle Puzzle on page 27. Don't forget to fill in the puzzle so you can see the secret message. The answers to all the puzzles (not that you'll need them) are at the end of the book.

The first Ponytail Girls book, *Meet the Ponytail Girls*, began just before school started in the fall. In *The Impossible Christmas Present*, you followed the PTs through the tragedies and triumphs of their holiday season. *Lost on Monster Mountain* saw the PTs off to Winter Camp with their Madison classmates. *A Stormy Spring* followed the PTs' adventures after returning from camp. *Escape from Camp Porcupine* takes them back to camp—this time in summer. *What's Up With Her?* explores all the joys and problems of a talent show. Who will be the winners?

The fun doesn't end with the stories. You can start your own Ponytail Girls Club. You can join by yourself, of course. But its much more fun if one of your friends joins with you. Or even five or six of them. There is no cost. You can read the Ponytail Girls stories together, do the puzzles and other activities, study the Bible stories and learn the Bible verses.

If your friends each have their own *Ponytail Girls* books, you can all write in yours at the same time. Arrange a regular meeting time and place and plan to do special things together, just like the PTs do in the stories, such as shopping, Bible study, homework, or helping others.

Meet Your Ponytail Girls!

· WHO ARE THEY? ·

The Ponytail Girls are eleven to thirteen year old girls who enjoy school, church, shopping, and being with their friends and family. They also love meeting new friends. Friends just like you! You'll love being a part of their lives.

The PTs all attend Madison Middle School in the small town of Circleville. They're all also members of Miss Kotter's Sunday school class at nearby Faith Church on Sunday mornings. On Sunday evenings, they attend the special Zone 56 youth group for guys and girls their age. Their pastor is Rev. J. T. McConahan, and their youth leader is Pastor Andrew Garretti, also known as "Pastor Andy."

Sam and Sara grew up in Circleville. Le's and LaToya's families moved into their neighborhood last year. When Sam and Sara met them at school, they invited them to church. Then Maria moved to Circleville and she became a PT, followed by Jenna and Brittany and Sonya. Now it would be hard for all of them to imagine not being PTs.

How did the PTs get their club name? Well, as you can see from their pictures, they all wear a ponytail of one kind or another. So that's what their other friends and families started calling them just for fun. Then one day LaToya shortened it to "PTs." Now that's what they all call themselves.

The PTs' club meetings are held whenever they can all get together. The girls have a secret motto: PT4JC, which means "Ponytails for Jesus Christ." They also have a secret code for the club's name: a "P" and a "T" back to back. But most of the time they don't want to keep secrets. They want to share with everyone the Good News about their best Friend, Jesus.

Have fun sharing in your PTs' adventures. Laugh with them in their silly times, think and pray with them through their problems, and learn with them that the answers to all problems can be found right in God's Word. Keep your Bible and a sharpened pencil handy. Sam and the others are waiting for you!

GET TO KNOW THE PTs

Sam Pearson *has a long blond ponytail, sparkling blue eyes, and a dream: she wants to play professional basketball. She also likes to design clothes. Sam's name is really "Samantha," but her friends and family just call her "Sam" for short. Sam's little brother, Petie, is 7. Joe, her dad, is great at fixing things, like cars and bikes, and runs the Superservice car repair shop. Her mom, Jean, bakes scrumptious goodies and works at the Paws and Pooches Animal Shelter. Sneezit is the tiny family dog and Sunlight is their kitten.*

LaToya Thomas' *black curls are ponytailed high above her ears. That way she doesn't miss a thing that's going on. LaToya's into gymnastics and playing the guitar. Her big sister, Tina, is a nurse. Her mom is a school teacher; her dad works with Mr. Pearson at Superservice. Also living with the Thomases is LaToya's beloved, wheelchair-bound grandmother, Granny B, and family kitten, Twilight.*

Le Tran *parts her glossy black hair to one side, holding it back with one small ponytail. She loves sewing, soccer, and playing the violin. Her mother, Viola, a concert pianist, often plays duets with her. Her father died in an accident, but became a Christian before he died. Le's mother is a new Christian. She has been dating Dr. Phan, music director at a Vietnamese church. He's a widower with two little boys, Michael and Nicolas. Le's kitten is Midnight.*

Sara Fields *lives down the street from Sam. She keeps her fiery red hair from flying away by tying it into a ponytail flat against each side of her head. Sara has freckles, glasses, and a great sense of humor. She loves singing, softball, ice skating, and cheerleading. Sara has a big brother, Tony, and a big dog, Tank, plus a kitten, Stormy. Her parents, Bob and Betsy, are artists.*

When **Maria Moreno** *moved in next door to Sam, she quickly became a PT, too. Maria pulls part of her long, brown hair into one topknot ponytail at the back; the rest hangs loose. She is tall, the way basketball-lover Sam would like to be. But Maria's into science and tennis, not basketball. At home, she helps her mother take care of her 6-year-old twin brothers, Juan and Ricardo, her little sister, Lolita, and the family kitten, Dinah-Mite. The Morenos all speak both English and Spanish.*

·Maria Moreno·

· Jenna Jenkins ·

Jenna Jenkins *is tall and wears her rich auburn ponytail high on her head, like a crown. Jenna loves ballet and tennis, her little sister Katie, and twin baby sisters, Noel and Holly, who were born at Christmas. Jenna's mom makes delicious cookies, and her dad is an accountant. Jenna's kitten is Skeeter Bite.*

Sonya Silverhorse *has a wheelchair and a warm smile. Her bouncy cocker spaniel's name is Cocky, and her kitten is Snow White. Sonya wears her coal-black ponytail long and braided, in honor of her Cherokee background. Her dad is Mr. Pearson's and Mr. Moreno's boss. Her mother died in the same accident that disabled Sonya. But Sonya loves to do things — like wheelchair basketball and playing the harmonica.*

Brittany Boorsma,
Madison's head cheerleader, was the prettiest girl at school, but she was also the most spiteful one — until she invited Christ into her heart. She pulls her long, naturally wavy blond hair together into a ponytail at her shoulder. Last winter she almost died in a blizzard. But God helped two dogs rescue her, and now Hope and Sweet Dreams are part of her family, too. Brittany plays the keyboard. Her father is an insurance agent.

Angie Andrews *is new in town, with a mother who has been quite sick and a father who is stationed over-seas. Shy and short, she wears a tiny ponytail in her long brown hair — off to the side with beads braided in it. She loves to draw and to help people.*

•Angie Andrews•

•Miss Kotter•

Miss Kitty Kotter, *the girls' Sunday school teacher, is not a PT, but she is an important part of their lives both in church and out of church. Miss Kotter works as a computer engineer. She also loves to go on hikes. Miss Kotter calls the Bible her "how-to book" because, she says, it tells "how to" live. Miss Kotter volunteers at the Circleville Rescue Mission.*

Get ready to have fun with the PTs!

Chapter 1

No End to Friends?

When Sam rushed in from school that Thursday afternoon, her little brother Petie almost knocked her down with excitement. "Sam, Sam! Guess what?" he cried. "Goldie just had puppies — you know, Mrs. Alvera's dog. And she said I could see them if you brought me over. Please, Sam, pretty please with sugar on it?"

Sam laughed. "Okay. As soon as I put my backpack down."

What adorable puppies! Four were gold-colored like their mother; the other was speckled brown and white. Oh, she just had to show them off to her PT friends.

"Mrs. Alvera," she asked, "may I please ask some of my friends over here to see the puppies after school tomorrow? We're all good at dog sitting. Maybe we can help you out with Goldie."

When her neighbor said yes, Sam could hardly wait to call the other PTs.

"Count me in," Sara replied. "I'll bring Maria and Le and LaToya."

"Good. I'll see if Jenna and Sonya and Brittany can come too. Puppies are so wonderful. I'm so glad God made puppies."

And she was even happier that God made friends. Sam had a lot of friends at Madison Middle School. She loved her teachers, too — well, most of them most of the time. As long as they didn't give pop quizzes. She definitely did not like pop quizzes.

She also had a lot of friends at Faith Church. She loved Pastor McConahan and their youth leader, Pastor Andy, and all the gang in Zone 56. And of course she loved her Sunday school teacher, Miss Kitty Kotter.

But her very best friends were the PTs: Sara, Jenna, Brittany, Maria, LaToya, Sonya, Le, and Jenna.

Just exactly the right number of friends. No, she didn't need any more. Not one more Ponytail Girl in their club. The PTs were perfect just the way they were!

After school on Friday, all the PTs crowded around Sam at her locker to go with her to see the puppies.

Sara ran up last. "Hey, gang!" she cried. "I just saw a poster outside Principal Anderson's office about a Talent Contest."

Circleville
Winner's Circle
Talent Contest
For All High School and Middle School Students!
Details next Monday!

"Details next Monday. Bummer." La Toya sighed. "I want the details now!"

Soon they were heading down the sidewalk toward Sam's street, toting backpacks, talking about the contest, telling jokes, giggling, even singing silly songs. Yes, there were no better friends in all the world than Sam and the PTs.

Even Miss Kotter was able to stop by the Alveras' after work to see the puppies. Mrs. Alvera met them all with a smile. "Come in, girls," she invited. "But please keep your voices down. Goldie's a little nervous. She's trying hard to be a good mother, you know."

At first Goldie growled at them. But when she saw her old friend Sam, a neighbor from across the street, she relaxed and wagged her tail. "Oh, Mrs. Alvera!" Le cried. "I've never had a puppy of my own. Do you think I could ask Mom for one?"

"Of course, dear, when they're older. Puppies make great friends. In fact, dogs are called 'man's best friend.' They're always there to protect us, comfort us, play with us, and keep us from getting lonely."

Outside, Sonya said, "Oh, guess what, everybody? I just got a letter from Red Wing — you know, the girl I met on the Cherokee reservation. She wants to be my friend. Isn't that sweet?"

Brittany nodded. "I just got an email from my cousin Nicole. Remember how snotty she used to be? Well, now she goes to church down in Florida. She apologized for the way she acted and wants to be friends."

Suddenly Sam wasn't half as happy. *Wait a minute!* she wanted to yell. *What's this business of more friends? We already have enough friends. We're the PTs. We're perfect just the way we are.*

But Miss Kotter was smiling. "I'm so glad you're making new friends, girls. That's how we can show God's love to others, by being friends with them. Just the way Ruth did in the Bible. I even have another new friend to introduce to all of you Sunday. Her name is Angie Andrews. She's new in town. Her mother's quite ill and her father is overseas in the Army. And yes, she wears a ponytail. Got room for one more in your club?"

No! Sam wanted to yell. *Let Angie go find her own friends.*

Then she thought of this poor girl, Angie. New in town, a sick mother, and a father overseas. Suddenly she was ashamed of herself; wasn't she acting exactly like a selfish brat? Well, yes — but it still wasn't fair. *Come on, God!* Sam cried. *Why are You making it so hard for me to do what's right? Can't you send Angie somewhere else and keep things just the way they were?*

She looked sadly at the other girls. Was this the end of her wonderful world of PTs?

· Good News · from God's Word

*Maybe you have lots of friends, like Sam.
Or maybe you don't have many and would like to have
more. Let's look at the life of Ruth and see what she did to
make friends when she moved to a brand-new place.*

Ruth Makes New Friends

FROM THE BOOK OF RUTH

Ruth loved her husband, his brother and wife, and her mother-in-law Naomi. They all lived in the land of Moab where Ruth had been born. She had many friends there and was very happy.

Then one day a sad thing happened. Both her husband and his brother died.

"I am too sad," sobbed Naomi. "I'm going to move back to Israel. You stay here with your family. You have many friends here. Maybe you'll marry again."

"Oh, no." Ruth protested. "God wants me to go with you."

So Ruth and Naomi traveled to Israel. Naomi already had friends here, but Ruth didn't. Yet God helped her make new friends. She went to work in the fields of a rich farmer. She got to know the other women who worked there. She was kind to all of them and became their friend. She even got to be friends with the rich farmer. And one day she married him.

All of this happened because Ruth was willing to trust God and reach out to others in love.

A Verse to Remember

"A friend loves at all times"

— ***Proverbs 17:17***

A Treasure Chest of Friends

Friends can be as precious as a treasure chest. They play with us, talk with us, help us, comfort us, help us make decisions. In the form below, list some or all of your friends. Then write down some ideas of how to show your appreciation to them — like help babysit, study with them, write them a note of thanks. Then put down the date that you actually did what you wanted to do. And don't forget to include your Best Friend of all — Jesus! You'll want to thank Him too.

FRIENDS	HOW TO THANK THEM	DATE
_____	_____	_____
_____	_____	_____
_____	_____	_____
_____	_____	_____
_____	_____	_____

The Winners Circle Puzzle

Some girls only want to think about God on Sunday mornings at church. The rest of the time they just want to think about new clothes or their homework or making lots of money or being popular or looking pretty.   But we need to put Jesus first every single day of the week. To solve this puzzle, write in the blanks the Secret Letters you will find at the end of each chapter in this book. For this chapter, write the letter "F" for "Friendly" in space #13. The final solution is on page 182.

Chapter 2

Giving Our Best

All Saturday the PTs kept calling each other about the Talent Contest. The kids were even talking about it Sunday morning at church. "The 4J2U Band just wrote a new song about Jesus," Josh said. "Maybe our band could play it for the Talent Contest. Wonder if that new girl Angie who's coming today would like to be in our band?"

And just like that, a perfectly gorgeous morning turned dark and gloomy. Angie Andrews! Sam had forgotten all about the new girl. Bummer. Was it too late to just turn around and go back home?

What if Angie didn't fit in? What if Sam didn't like her? Even worse, what if Miss Kitty liked Angie better than the others?

Up to now her Sunday school class was just perfect. Everyone in it was a PT. All the girls were Christians who loved the Lord. Surely God didn't want that to change. Not if He wanted the best for Sam, right?

Just then she got a hug from behind. "Maria" she laughed.

Maria glowed. "Buenos Días, girl. Ready to meet a new PT?" she asked.

Sam tried to grin back. "Good morning yourself. I'm always ready for something new." But was she really?

Just as they reached their classroom, Sonya wheeled in. A new girl was beside her: Angie.

Angie was very short with long, straight brown hair. And, yes, she did have a ponytail — a tiny one on one side, with beads braided in it. She looked very shy and very nervous.

Miss Kitty introduced their new class member. Then she told the Bible story from Exodus about how it wasn't just men who helped get the Tabernacle ready for God, but women too.

"Sometimes we girls think we are not good enough for God," Miss Kitty said. "We think we need to be richer or prettier or smarter. Sometimes people tell us that girls can't do anything important. But we can. You see, God made us just the way we are. He loves us just the way we are. And He wants to help us give our very best for Him."

Angie raised her hand shyly. "I miss my Dad very much," she said. "But he's overseas giving his best for his country. I want to give my best too, to make him proud of me. But I don't know what I can do. And I worry about my Mom. She has heart problems. I wish she'd get better."

Le hugged Angie. "Let's pray for your Mom right now. And pray that we'll all give our best." So they all joined in.

Sam felt very ashamed. Not wanting to be Angie's friend was not giving her best to God or to Angie, either. She gave the new girl a hug, too. "Welcome to our class, Angie," she said. "And welcome to Faith Church. And welcome to Madison Middle School. And to the PTs, too. We're so glad you came."

Angie sat with them in church. Afterward, they all gathered around her, telling about their school that she would enroll in on Monday. And the big city-wide Talent Contest.

"Maria is great in science," Sam said. "Sara's a fab ice skater. Jenna does ballet. LaToya's into gymnastics. All of us can do something. I think I'll try basketball or do some special tricks with Sneezit. So what's your talent, Angie?"

The new girl shrugged her shoulders sadly. "Nothing, I guess. About the only thing I like to do is draw, and I can't do that on stage. So don't worry about me. I guess I just don't fit in."

Maria gave her a hug. "You fit in just fine, Angie. You even have a ponytail. And I think it's wonderful you can draw. Sara's folks are artists. They'd love to meet you. What do you think, Sam?"

Sam blushed. She really hadn't wanted Angie to fit in. Actually, Sam wanted her to just go away and disappear. But suddenly she wanted Angie to stay — and to be a real PT.

"I'd like to see some of your artwork, Angie," she replied. "Who knows? Maybe we could work that into the Talent Contest, too. What do you think?"

Angie smiled shyly. "Well, maybe. At least I could try, couldn't I?"

Sam hugged her. "You'll do great, I know it."

Okay, God, Sam prayed. *Now what do I do next? I said that just to make her feel good. But what if drawing doesn't fit into the contest, no matter how good it is? Then how are You going to get me out of this mess?*

· Good News ·
from God's Word

Angie wasn't sure if doing her best drawing would be good enough. But God can always use our best if we ask Him to help us. Here are some women who gave their best — and helped build God's House.

Women Who Helped Build
the Tabernacle

EXODUS 35:21-29

After God's people, the Israelites, were rescued from Egypt, they wandered around in the desert on their way to the Promised Land. The

Promised Land was another name for the nation of Israel. God had been promising it as a home to His people for hundreds of years. That's where God told Moses to take His people. It would be their new home.

God's people wanted a place to worship Him. But they couldn't build a church or temple out in the desert. Besides, they were always traveling. They lived in tents that they could set up and take down and carry with them. They needed a church-tent they could take with them, too. So God told them how to make one. They called this special tent for worship the Tabernacle.

They needed large trees to make the tent poles. They needed very large curtains to be the roof and the sides. They needed wood and metal for all the furniture, and fine garments for the priests to wear. And someone needed to make them all right out there in the desert.

The men, of course, were glad to volunteer. But so were the women. The Bible tells us they brought their jewelry to be melted down for the Tabernacle needs. They brought yarn and cloth and goat hair and dyed furs and leather. All the precious materials they had carefully carried with them on their trip they now gave to God for His new House.

The Bible also tells us that the women spun new yarns and cloth and dyed them, yards and yards of them, because the Tabernacle was so big. The Bible calls them "skilled women." They were women who had learned how to do something and were glad to use their talents for the Lord — glad to give Him their very best.

A Verse to Remember

"God has the power to help"

— **2 Chronicles 25:8**

Being the Best They Could Be

These Bible women did their best for God. See if you can figure out from this list of names which woman belongs with each quote.

Names: Lydia, Miriam, Rhoda, Esther, Mary, Deborah, Dorcas

1. I stood beside the river Nile.
   A princess came by after a while.
   Who am I? _____

2. I became a beautiful Queen
   Who saved my people from
   Haman mean.
   Who am I? _____

3. I made clothes for the poor. And when
   I died, Peter brought me to life again.
   Who am I? _____

4. An angel told me I'd have a Son.
   Jesus of Nazareth, He's the One.
   Who am I? _____

5. I was a seller of purple dye.
   I believed in Jesus when Paul
   came by.
   Who am I? _____

6. When an angel from jail set Peter free,
   Who answered the door when he knocked? Yes, me.
   Who am I? _____

7. I was a prophetess, judge, and more —
   I led God's army down Mt. Tabor.
   Who am I? _____

The Winners Circle Puzzle

Add Secret Letter "G" for "giving her best" in space 7 of the puzzle.

Chapter 3

That's Not Fair!

Everyone stopped by to see the new puppies again that afternoon. "Which one's the cutest?" Jenna asked. "Maybe we need a puppy contest."

Miss Kitty laughed. "I have a better idea. What about an Old Folks Contest?"

Brittany wiggled her nose. "Old Folks? You mean, to find out who's the oldest person around?"

"My Great-Grandma Silverhorse lived to be 96," Sonya announced. "But she's with Jesus now."

Miss Kitty laughed again. "Oh, no, no, no, that's not what I mean. I mean, tomorrow at school you're going to find out all about the new Circleville Talent Contest for Teens and Tweens. Did you know that older people have talents, too? When I first volunteered down at the Whispering Pines Nursing Home, I found out that the patients love to sing. They love to write. Maybe they have other talents, too — like knitting or chess or playing instruments. Why don't we have a Senior Circle Contest and see what we come up with?"

Sam looked at LaToya and LaToya looked at Maria. "Uh, that's nice, Miss Kitty," Sam said finally. "Maybe we can do it after our own Talent Contest is over. But we're going to be pretty busy till then."

Le nodded. "Yes, I'm going to have to practice my violin a lot more. Maybe I can do one classical piece and one hillbilly hoedown for the Contest."

"I'll double my practice time," Jenna agreed. "Maybe I can find someone to do a ballet duet with me."

"Oh, yes, of course," their teacher murmured. But she looked a little sad.

The next morning half the school crowded around Principal Anderson's office waiting to see if they would put up a new poster about the Contest.

Finally his secretary, Miss Bernstein, poked her head
out the door. "Shoo." she yelled. "On to your home
rooms before the floor falls through from your
weight. Your home room teachers have all the info
about the Contest you need. So now let's see what
talent you have for finding your home rooms before
the tardy bell rings. Shoo."

Maria's home room teacher passed out flyers
about the Contest to everyone. She and Le grinned
when they read them.

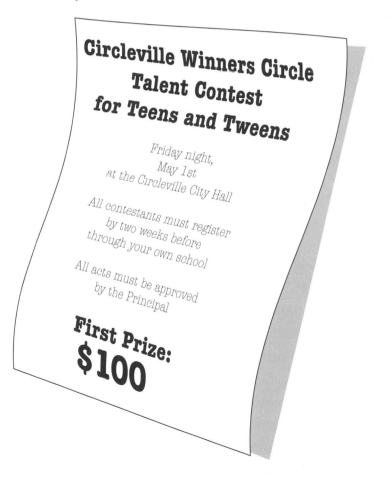

**Circleville Winners Circle
Talent Contest
for Teens and Tweens**

Friday night,
May 1st,
at the Circleville City Hall

All contestants must register
by two weeks before
through your own school

All acts must be approved
by the Principal

**First Prize:
$100**

Josh whistled. "$100! That settles it. I'm signing up today."

The next few days were a madhouse. LaToya signed up for gymnastics. Right off she had a gymnastics meet and won. Sonya's team won in wheelchair basketball. Sara won at an ice skating meet. Jenna found a ballet partner and they practiced every day. Sam decided to teach Sneezit to do tricks.

"See, the PTs are going to win everything." Sam announced. "The PTs are the greatest!"

But then ...

... Sonya's basketball coach lost his job and moved away. LaToya sprained her ankle. Sara's skates were stolen. Sneezit decided he definitely did not want to learn new tricks. Brittany fell during a cheerleading routine and had to hobble around on crutches. Maria got behind in her science project.

Now Sam moaned, "The PTs are never going to win anything. We're doomed. We might as well all give up."

That Sunday morning Miss Kitty told the Bible story of Lot's wife. "Times were hard for her," the teacher said, "but God had a way out for her. She didn't have to give up. She didn't have to look back and have a pity party. God wanted her to have the courage to look ahead, even when times were hard. And God wants that for you girls, too. Maybe, you know, God wants you to take your eyes off the Contest for a while and think of pleasing Him by helping others."

Instantly Brittany stopped smiling. And she was still grumpy when they sat down in church. "Stop thinking of the Contest?" she fumed. "That's impossible! I want to think about it every minute and win it."

"My thoughts exactly," Sam cried. "Why does Miss Kitty have to dump on us and make us feel guilty? It's hard enough to do all our chores and our homework and everything and practice for the Contest, too."

Maria nodded. "I know just how you feel. I want to do good — but I want to win in the Contest. I want to help these old people, but I want to help me too. I don't know what to do now — do you?"

· Good News · from God's Word

It's easy to feel sorry for ourselves when things don't go the way we planned, right? And just as easy to forget to ask God for His help. Which is exactly what happened to Lot's wife.

Lot's Wife Looks Back

FROM GENESIS 19:1-26

"Hurry!" cried the angel. "You must leave at once. Your city Sodom is so evil, God is going to have to punish it with a great earthquake and lava.

But since you believe in God, God wants to spare you. But you must obey us and leave!"

Lot looked at his wife and daughters. "But I don't want to leave," he said. "I have friends here."

"I have friends here, too," cried his wife. "And my family. I like this city. I love the stores and the food and the parties. Why should we leave?"

Finally the angels grabbed their hands and led them out of the city.

"Now, run as fast as you can" the angels urged. "Don't stop till you reach the mountains."

"But I can't run fast" Lot cried. "I'm not used to running. Can't we stay in a small village that is near by instead?"

"All right," said the angel. "But hurry."

Lot and his daughters hurried to the village. But not Lot's wife. She was too sad and angry. "It's not fair!" she said. "I like living in Sodom. I miss it already." So instead of going ahead with her family, she sat there and looked back at the city, having a real pity party. Crying for her city and being so mad at God, she refused to move.

So her husband and daughters rushed on without her. Just as they reached the village, all the earthquakes and lava started. Lot's city was destroyed. His family was safe — but not his wife. Burning sulfur filled the air — and soon she was covered all over with a thick layer of mineral salts. Just like that she was dead. All because she would rather have a pity party than obey God and be safe.

A Verse to Remember

"Obey the Lord your God"

— *Jeremiah 26:13*

The PTs' 411

This quiz checks to see how well you know your Ponytail Girls friends. If this is your first PT book, many of the answers are found in the first five books in the series as well as in the *Meet Your Ponytail Girls* section beginning on page 11. Here are the names of the PTs: Sam, Le, Maria, LaToya, Sonya, Jenna, Brittany, Sara, and the newest girl, Angie.

1. Brittany plays the electric

2. Sam has a dog named

3. LaToya's grandmother is called

4. Jenna has two little twin

5. Sam's dad works for an

6. Le plays the

7. Maria speaks English and

8. Sam's neighbor's dog just had

9. The PTs go to this school

10. Sara's parents are

11. The newest PT is named

12. Sonya plays wheelchair

13. Miss Kitty's last name is

A. puppies

B. Spanish

C. Kotter

D. Madison Middle

E. artists

F. basketball

G. Sneezit

H. keyboard

I. Granny B

J. auto company

K. sisters

L. violin

M. Angie

Good-Bye to Pity Parties

Did you ever feel sorry for yourself? Did you think your parents weren't being fair, that God wasn't being fair? You didn't like what you saw in the mirror? You didn't like your clothes or hair color or freckles? Pity parties don't help anything. If you want to look better, brush your hair and smile. Instead of holing up in your room, try to obey your parents and be their friend. Instead of blaming God, ask Him to help you do better and be better. He will!

The Winners Circle Puzzle

Add Secret Letter "N" for "no pity parties" to space 6 of the puzzle.

Chapter 4

Senior Moments

"Well, guess what, everyone" Miss Kitty announced as she walked into Sam's living room the next afternoon. "Guess who's now out of work? Unemployed? A has-been? Me!"

"What?" all the girls cried. This was supposed to be a planning meeting for the old folks' Talent Contest — the one they didn't really want to have. "What happened?"

"Well, my company merged with another firm recently. Now they're moving the computer section

47

to Detroit. They never came out and told us this would happen, but I suspected as much, and I've been looking for a job around here, just in case." She sighed. "But most of the companies around here are either subcontracting to another local computer firm or they're outsourcing everything overseas."

Petie was behind the couch, playing his Gameboy. He popped his head up. "Does that mean you'll be broke and get kicked out of your apartment, Miss Kitty? You can come live with us. Sam's got bunkbeds. 'Course she's always got a huge mess of clothes on the floor, but you can step on them to reach the top bunk."

Everyone laughed except for Sam. "No, dear," Miss Kitty replied. "However, if I don't find a job in this area soon, I'll have to move to a larger town like Summer City. Or even farther away. I'd hate for that to happen. I love living in Circleville. But I'm trusting in the Lord. He's the one who has all the answers."

Then they turned back to the reason for their meeting. Sam pulled the calendar off the fridge door and Miss Kitty called the Whispering Pines activities director to see about an available date for a Talent Contest for their residents.

"It's all settled." She smiled as she hung up the phone. "We'll go over Wednesday after school to talk with the residents and get them signed up. Then the following Saturday we'll have the Seniors' Circle contest."

Everyone smiled back—at least on the outside. But under her breath Brittany muttered, "And then we can get back to the important contest — the one at school."

The activities director at Whispering Pines was short and plump and glowing with smiles when the PTs arrived on Wednesday. "Welcome, welcome, girls. Thanks for coming. I've assigned each of you some room numbers to talk to the residents.

And here's a notepad and pen for each of you to write down the information. I've already put up posters about the contest all over the home. So I know our residents are really going to be excited."

Well, some were, some weren't. But as the girls went from room to room, the senior citizens began warming up. "I used to whistle when I was younger," confided one old lady. "I even whistled on the radio. Wonder if I still can?"

"I used to wear a braid just like yours," one confided to Sonya.

"I can set up a mean domino sculpture," announced a man. "Yep. I can set them up around this whole room and have them knock each other down, one by one, in two seconds. Used to be a champ, you know."

Others wrote poetry or played checkers or told funny jokes or sang. One old lady played the banjo and a couple did ballroom dancing. One did crossword puzzles in ink and never made a mistake. And one had turned his wheelchair into a complete band, with drums, harmonica, and more.

By the time Saturday came, all the residents were excited. And so were the PTs. Brittany volunteered to play her keyboard for the singers. Even Granny B came along to help lead the singing. Miss Kitty acted as the emcee. And a reporter from the Circleville Sentinel was there for the whole thing. So was a news reporter from Channel 7. Even some of the guys from Zone 56 came to cheer them on.

Some acts were just funny. Others were wonderful. Yes, that old lady still could whistle as clear as bells — even though she was now 96. And when one of the men read a story he wrote about growing up in a very poor but loving family, there wasn't a dry eye in the place.

"You're never too old for life and love," said the reporter afterwards, as they all shared cake and ice cream. "Or too young to help others. Thanks, kids. I know you have a Talent Contest coming up for your own age. But thanks for being interested in others and willing to help them."

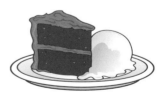

And Miss Kitty gave them all a big wink.

Brittany winked back. *Okay, Talent Contest. Here I come!*

· Good News · from God's Word

Just as the residents of Whispering Pines were much older than the PTs, so Elizabeth in this next story was much older than her young relative, Mary. But that didn't stop them from being great friends.

Mary and Elizabeth Help Each Other

LUKE 1:39-56

Mary had the most wonderful news. It was a secret told her by an angel: she was going to have a baby. Not just any baby, but God's only special Son. Now that really was news!

She was dying to share her news with someone. But who? Her girl friends in the village of

Nazareth might not understand. They might even make fun of her and her fiancé Joseph, and accuse them of doing naughty things, or of making the whole thing up. She needed to talk to someone who would understand.

And then she remembered her relative Elizabeth. Elizabeth was an older woman — old enough to be Mary's grandmother. But she was kind and loving. Her husband, Zechariah, was a priest and both of them loved God and believed God's Word. Both of them were looking forward to when God would send His Son into the world.

And guess what? Elizabeth was expecting a baby, too. Yes, even though she was old enough to be a grandmother. Her baby would be a very special miracle just as Mary's baby would be a miracle. Elizabeth was the perfect one to talk to.

So Mary packed up some lunches and extra clothes and set out for the trip. We don't know if she walked or rode a donkey. But Elizabeth's home in the mountains of Judea was 35 to 40 miles away. That was a long way to walk. And there were no motels to stay in along the way, and no McDonald's to stop by for lunch.

But finally she reached Elizabeth's home. God blessed them both. God told Elizabeth all about Mary's baby. And God helped Mary instantly make up and sing a glorious hymn of praise.

Mary stayed there three months, until it was time for Elizabeth's baby to come. That baby became the great prophet and preacher, John the Baptist, who helped lead many people to Jesus. In fact, one day he baptized Jesus.

How glad Mary was that she and Elizabeth took time to help each other and to encourage each other.

A Verse to Remember

"Each of you should look not only to your own interests, but also to the interests of others."
— **Philippians 2:4**

You Can Help, Too
Word Search Puzzle

Here are some of the ways you can help those who need a friend, such as a lonely old person, someone with disabilities, a new mother, or one with several children. See how many of these words you can find in the puzzle. Remember that the words go up, down, backwards, and forwards.

How many of these ways to help do you do? Can you think of more ways to help?

Wash car	**pet sitting**	**housework**
talk	(for them)	(for them)
write	**shopping**	(help children with)
(letters for them)	(for them)	**homework**
visit	**baby sitting**	**water** (lawn)
read (to them)	**lawn work**	**take tapes**
pray (for them)	**hug** (them)	(to them)
take food	**go**	**phone** (them)
(to them)		

```
B  W  A  S  H  C  A  R  H  H  X
A  P  H  O  N  E  L  X  O  O  S
B  G  O  X  K  L  A  T  U  M  E
Y  U  R  E  T  A  W  X  S  E  P
S  H  O  P  P  I  N  G  E  W  A
I  X  E  T  I  R  W  P  W  O  T
T  I  S  I  V  X  O  H  O  R  E
T  X  X  D  A  E  R  O  R  K  K
I  P  R  A  Y  X  K  T  K  X  A
N  T  A  K  E  F  O  O  D  X  T
G  P  E  T  S  I  T  T  I  N  G
```

Puzzle answers begin on page 182.

The Winners Circle Puzzle

Add Secret Letter "I" for "interested in others" in space 5 of the puzzle.

Chapter 5

All for One and One for All?

"It's just not fair!" Brittany grumped to Mrs. Perez, her drama teacher. "The doctor says I have to use these nasty old crutches for another two weeks. How am I ever going to get to practice my cheerleading routines for the Talent Contest? I'm doomed."

Mrs. Perez laughed. "Oh, Brittany. Why don't you do a monologue — you know, it's like a play that you do all by yourself? You know you're a natural for drama. You can practice it even on crutches, and by the time the Contest is here, you won't need your crutches any more. I have several books on monologues here in my desk, and we have more in the school library. You can even write your own — funny or serious. What do you think?"

Brittany swirled her yellow ponytail. "I think you're looking at a stand-up comic," she giggled. "Even if I have to be a sit-down one. Any special monologue you'd recommend?"

Soon they found a very funny one about a doll named Polly Wood who wanted to go to Hollywood. Brittany was surprised to find out she could memorize it so easily. Soon she knew the whole thing by heart.

"Oh, Brittany" cried Mrs. Perez. "You're a natural at this. I can't believe how well you're doing. Look, I want your mother to call me. There's a photographer I'd like her to meet. I think you should get a portfolio together. Then I'll help you find a talent agent."

Brittany's head was spinning at that. Talent agent! Maybe she'd really be in the movies. Hollywood — that's a long way from Circleville. But she'd never forget her PT friends when she was famous. She'd even invite them out to California to see her studio. She could almost see her name up in lights!

With her head full of dreams, she almost ran right into her cheerleading team.

"Brittany!" Brooke cried. "Where have you been? And why are you still using those stupid crutches?"

"Yeah" barked Rachel. "How are we going to get our cheerleading routines down for the Talent Contest without you?"

"We almost think you're trying to avoid us," Jennifer sighed. "Brit, gal, we need you. Don't desert us now."

"Oh, uh, I'm not deserting," she shot back. "I'll be there as soon as the doctor lets me off these stupid crutches." But suddenly, after hearing what Mrs. Perez said, she wasn't sure he ever wanted to waste her time cheerleading again. Not when she could be a movie star.

What should she do? Who could advise her? Why, Miss Kitty, of course.

Pulling out her cell phone, she dialed her teacher's number. "Miss Kitty, I've got a problem. Can you help me?"

"Sure, dear. Why don't you meet me at Burger Basket after school and we'll talk?"

Good old Miss Kitty. When classes were over, Brittany grabbed her backpack and hobbled down the street. Would Miss Kitty be sitting at a table or at a booth?

But when she walked inside, surprise! She wasn't at either one. She was behind the counter — working.

"Hi, Brittany," she said. "What's up? You look shocked to see me back here. Well, I needed a temporary job and they just happened to have one available. Now, what's your problem?

After Brittany told her, her teacher smiled. "Brittany, you don't want to disappoint your friends. As soon as the doctor lets you, be sure to practice with them again. That way you can be a winning team. But keep up the monologue practice, too. You can enter in both events at the Talent Contest.

"But I'd hold off on the photo shoots and stuff. First, see how your comic act goes in public. Meanwhile, I'll be praying for you to heal and do well.

And you can pray for me to find the new job of God's choosing. That's what true friends do, right — help each other?" Then nodding to the door, she said, "Oops, here comes another customer. Gotta go."

"Me, too, Miss Kitty, thanks. I'm glad God made friends. Especially friends like you."

Then she looked down at her crutches and up at her teacher — a computer expert flipping hamburgers. *Okay, God, how are You going to get us both out of this mess?*

· Good News ·
from God's Word

Brittany and Miss Kitty both found they
needed really true friends when the going was rough
— not just people who pretended to be friends. So did
a young girl named Esther.

Esther and Her Cousin: True Friends
THE BOOK OF ESTHER

Both of Esther's parents died when she was a
little girl, so one of her cousins adopted her. His
name was Mordecai. He tried to be a good father to
her. He taught her right from wrong, and to love
God and His Word.

Esther grew up to be a beautiful young woman. So beautiful, in fact, that the King wanted to marry her. Now this King had a strange name, Xerxes (pronounced Zerk-zeez). He was king of a faraway land called Persia, and was very rich and powerful.

Mordecai's family had come to Persia many years before from the land of Israel. He was a Jew. Esther was a Jew, too. But most people didn't know that. They just thought that Esther and Mordecai were Persians like everyone else.

Mordecai was a very brave man, and helped save the life of the King. The King was glad to honor him. And he was glad to marry the beautiful Esther. They were all very happy.

But someone wasn't happy — a mean man named Haman. He knew that Mordecai was a Jew, so he and his friends figured out a way to try to kill all the Jews, to get revenge on Mordecai. Mordecai told his cousin, the new Queen. "It is up to you to save the Jews," he told her.

It took a lot of courage and a lot of tact and a lot of thinking things through. But Esther did save her people. The evil Haman got his punishment, and the Jews ever since have been celebrating the Feast of Purim in honor of a brave young Queen and her cousin.

A Verse to Remember

"Do not forsake your friend."

— **Proverbs 27:10**

Her Name in Lights!

Color all the circles that have B in them and you'll see how Brittany imagined her name would look in lights if she became famous.

Puzzle answers begin on page 182.

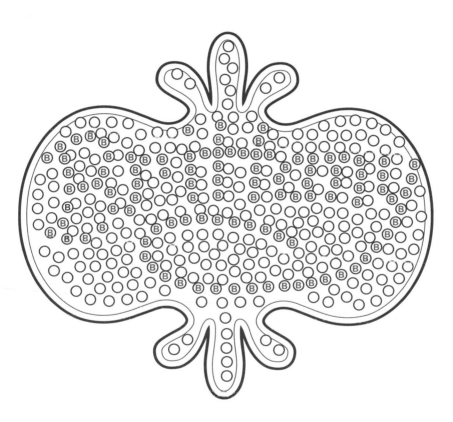

The Winners Circle Puzzle

Add Secret Letter "T" for "true friend" in space 17 of the puzzle.

Chapter 6

What About Angie?

Dr. Willnow laughed as he looked at the x-rays of Brittany's leg. "All right, young lady. You're now ready to ditch those crutches and get on with your life."

Yea! She dove right back in to her monologue and cheerleading practice. LaToya's ankle was better too, so she was now back into gymnastics. She won another meet, besides playing guitar with the 4J2U praise band. She really loved Josh and Kevin's new song, "He's Reaching Out His Hand." It would be so cool to play it in the Talent Contest as a witness to the other students and their families.

Jenna and her ballet partner, Alyce, had created their own routine called "Song of the Daffodil." Sam and Sonya helped design costumes for them. Sonya's dad was now the wheelchair basketball coach, and they'd already won one game. Le had memorized one piece by Mozart for the violin — plus a real country fiddle version of "Turkey in the Straw." Sara got new skates and practiced her ice skating every day. Maria was going to tell a story about her great-grandparents in Mexico.

"But, Sam" her little brother Petie asked, puzzled. "Are you really going to have a skate rink in the City Hall? Are people really going to play basketball there? Besides, what are you going to do in the Contest?"

She laughed. "People can either do something live on stage or show videos of what they did somewhere else. As for me, I still don't know. I was going to do tricks with Sneezit, but he wouldn't have anything to do with it."

"You could do tricks with me, Sis," Petie replied. " I know some real neat ones. Dad taught them to me and I got a book to learn some more. I bet

Sneezit would okay it if I helped. I think the three of us could make a great team. Want to try?"

"Wow, Petie! What a neat idea. First I need to find out if you can participate, 'cause you're not really old enough. If they say okay, we're on"

She gave him a big high five.

When Principal Anderson gave his okay, Sam couldn't wait to call LaToya and tell her the news.

"That's great, Sam. I guess all the PTs are going to enter now. Do you know what Angie's going to do?"

"Angie?" Oops. Sam had forgotten all about

Angie. "Uh, I'll give her a call."

But when Sam reached their new friend, she was crying so hard she could hardly talk. "Oh, Sam," she sobbed, "please pray for my mom. You know she has heart problems. And last night the paramedics rushed her to the Midland Hospital. They wouldn't let me come along, and I'm so scared for her."

Sam couldn't believe it. "You mean you're home all by yourself? What about your Grandma or some other relative coming to stay with you?"

"They all live back in Pennsylvania. And Dad's overseas in the Army. But the worst part of it is no one at the hospital will tell me anything when I call to ask about Mom. They say that's confidential information. I-I don't even know if she's still alive." Her sobs grew louder.

"Don't worry, Angie," Sam said. "We're going to help."

Right after that, Sam called LaToya back. LaToya's big sister, Tina, was a nurse at Midland Hospital, so she'd be able to help at that end. Then Sam called and left a message on Miss Kitty's phone about Angie, and on the church phone to let Pastor McConahan know. Proud of herself for being such a good helper, she started sketching her and Petie's costumes for their trick show.

That night at dinner when Sam told her mother about Angie, Mrs. Pearson was horrified. "Sam!" she cried. "We can't let that poor girl stay over there by herself."

Sam helped herself to some more spaghetti. "Oh, she'll be fine. Miss Kitty will take care of her. That's her job, isn't it?"

Her mother frowned. "Shame on you, Samantha. Didn't you know that Miss Kotter is out of town for a job interview? Extending a helping hand is everybody's job. We need to feed that girl and get her a place to stay and get her mom's name on the church's prayer chain right away. We need to show her we love her, and that Jesus loves her too."

So the PTs and their parents went into action. Mrs. Pearson and Sam brought Angie over to eat dinner, then took her to the hospital to see her Mom. Tina and Pastor McConahan met them there. Her mother was better, but would have to stay for a few days. How glad she was to know that her daughter was all right.

Sara's folks took Angie home to stay with them until her mother was released. When Angie saw their paintings and drawings, she was thrilled. "I want to be an artist, too," she said. "I want to draw a picture of Goldie's puppies for the Talent Contest."

They hugged her. "We'll help you, Angie," they said. "We have all the art supplies you need. And we'll even show you how to use them"

Angie hugged them back. "Oh, that's wonderful. Maybe I can even draw a picture of Mom and send it to my dad overseas. Could you help me do that, too?"

· Good News · from God's Word

What's the difference between just saying, "Have a nice day," and really helping someone? Sam learned the difference — and so did King Saul's daughter in this story.

Michal Helps David

1 SAMUEL 16-19

Saul was King of Israel. But he was not a good king. He was very proud, and he didn't like to have to obey God. Finally God told the Prophet Samuel that God had chosen a new king for His people — the young shepherd boy, David.

David stayed out in the fields with the sheep.

But he spent his time there making up hymns and praising God. He had a lovely voice and carried a small harp around with him to play.

Saul knew that God wasn't pleased with him. But instead of telling God he was sorry, he kept getting angrier and angrier, which made him sick and miserable. "Maybe listening to quiet music would make him feel better," decided his servants. So they set up a search — sort of like a talent contest. And that's how they found young David and brought him to the palace.

Everyone liked David, including the king. He hired him on the spot. After that, whenever the king felt miserable, David would play for him and make him better. The king's daughter Michal liked to hear him too, because she had fallen in love with him.

Then the mean giant Goliath threatened all of God's people. Everyone was too afraid to fight him — except for young David. He fought and won. After that, the king let David marry his daughter Michal. But now the king didn't like David as much. The king was too jealous. He tried to kill David. He even tried to kill him at David's house.

But Michal loved David too much to let that happen. She helped him escape down a window, by a rope or a sheet, then put a dummy in David's bed. When Saul tried to kill him this time, David was long gone.

Michal felt bad that her father was so cruel. But she was glad God helped her save the life of her husband.

A Verse to Remember

*"She opens her arms to the poor
and extends her hands to the needy"*

— Proverbs 31:20

Tons of Talent Crossword Puzzle

See if you can discover some of the categories the PTs and their friends are entering for the big Talent Contest. Puzzle answers begin on page 182.

DOWN:

1. New costumes may _____ a lot of money
3. Petie could do one of these
5. Like a one-person play
7. LaToya plays one (a country-western instrument)
8. If I'm not you, I must be _____
9. Sonya plays wheelchair _____
11. Athletes like to _____ trophies by doing their best
14. Le plays one (also called a fiddle)
15. This is a nickname for Michael

ACROSS:

2. Like singing with your mouth closed
4. LaToya trains to be one of these, doing gymnastics

6. When a band performs it's called a _____

10. These teams help lead cheers

12. Street (abbreviation)

13. Abbreviation for Arkansas

16. This is done on ice

17. Jenna is good at this kind of dance

18. Everyone likes to _____ contests

The Winners Circle Puzzle

Add Secret Letter "E" for "extending a helping hand" to space 9 of the puzzle.

Chapter 7

Oh, You Beautiful Doll!

"No, no, Sam!" her little brother Petie
protested. "That's not how to do this trick. Move
your fingers like this, not like that. Otherwise, people
will be able to see what you're doing, and that won't
be any fun at all."

"Yeah, sorry. I'll try again."

Sam liked learning the magic tricks. What she didn't like was having to learn them from her own little brother. It made her feel so stupid. She should be teaching him things instead.

Just then the phone rang. "Sam, it's Angie. Guess what? My mom's better. She might even get to come home from the hospital tomorrow. Miss Kitty just got back in town, and she went over to visit Mom today. And when she's home from the hospital, LaToya's sister Tina is going to come over every day to check on her. I love being here with Sara's family. But I can hardly wait to go back home and be with Mom and be our own family again.

"Oh, by the way, could you ask your neighbor if it's okay if I come over and take some pictures of her puppies? I'll use them to make my sketches for the Talent Contest. And I'll give her copies of the finished pictures when I'm done."

Mrs. Alvera was thrilled to have Angie over. And Sam's mom was thrilled to know that Mrs. Andrews was doing better. "But she's going to need a lot of help when she comes home," Mrs. Pearson said. "She'll have to stay in bed a few days. I'll contact

everyone about sending food over to her to help out. Oh, Sam, could you see who's at the front door?"

It was the UPS delivery man — with a large package addressed to Sam. And it was too big for her to pick up.

She ran to her mother. "It's from Aunt Irene in Detroit. Wonder what it is?"

"Hey!" Petie said. "Why don't you open it and find out? Maybe it's a big box of chocolate chip cookies."

Instead, it was all her aunt's old dolls — the ones she herself had played with as a girl. Aunt Irene had only sons, so she was passing them on to her niece. "I know you always loved dolls, too," her aunt wrote.

Yes, but Sam was in Middle School now — a little too old to play with dolls. And these dolls weren't fancy collectibles to put away in a cabinet or sell on e-bay. They were just plain, ordinary, well-loved and used dolls with rather dull, worn clothes on. Twenty of them. What in the world should Sam do with them without hurting Aunt Irene's feelings?

"Maybe your PT friends will have an idea," Mom suggested. So Sam called Sonya.

"Oh, I do have an idea" Sonya cried. "Remember how you and I have been taking design classes? And how we made clothes for ourselves? What if we design and make clothes for these dolls? Then we can put on a Doll Fashion Show at the Talent Contest. And have Angie take pictures of them to send back to your aunt."

"Wow, Sonya!" Sam cried. "What an ingenious idea. Helping them disappear into loving arms of little girls will be the best trick of all. Okay, Sonya, what do you say — another First Prize in the Contest coming up?"

· Good News · from God's Word

What do you think it would feel like to be the very first girl in the world? Without a school or store or even a comb? Hard, right? On the other hand, no traffic jams or report cards!

Adam and Eve's Daughters

GENESIS 3:1-5:4

Everyone has heard of Cain and Abel and Seth, Adam and Eve's first sons. But guess what? They had daughters, too. In fact, eventually they had lots of sons and lots of daughters.

Did you ever think of what like must have been like in the very first home? Where do you keep your clothes? Yes, in closets and chests of drawers. But the first family didn't have anything like that. In fact, every single thing they put on had to be made first — by them. And all their furniture too.

If they wore fur in the winter to keep warm, someone had to kill an animal, and then clean and cut the fur. That meant making their own knives too — maybe out of bone. If they wore leather sandals, they first had to tan the leather, and then make the shoes. If they wore cloth in the hot summers, they had to grow the cotton or linen, then prepare it for spinning into thread and then weave the thread into cloth. And they had to make needles to sew it with.

And that's not all. They had to grow their own food and make their own pots and their own dishes to eat with. They had to weave their own blankets to sleep under, and make their own pillows. They even had to make their own tent to live in.

Adam and the men worked hard. But Eve and her daughters worked hard, too. They had lots to do, but maybe some of it was fun. What was it like to invent the very first pot? What was it like to bake the very first cake? Or produce the very first pair of socks? What was it like to make cradles for baby brothers and sisters and babysit them? What was it

like to be homeschooled without books? To never go to the mall, never get a letter in the mail, never go visit your grandparents?

Yes, some of life was hard. But they had each other. And God helped them have ideas and figure out how to make all they needed. They were ingenious. They probably even made toys and games. In fact, in just a few generations people were creating musical instruments and making all kinds of metal tools.

Aren't you glad that when we're faced with problems, God can help us find the solutions — just as He helped Eve and her daughters?

A Verse to Remember

"She ... works with eager hands"

— **Proverbs 31:13**

Ready for the Fashion Show

Pretend this is one of the dolls Aunt Irene sent to Sam. Try designing an outfit for her that would be fun to enter into Sam's Doll Fashion Show.

The Winners Circle Puzzle

Add Secret Letter "I" for "ingenuity" in space 14 of the puzzle.

Chapter 8

Ark in the Park

Maria curled up on the couch doing her homework while her little sister Lolita stared out the window. Outside the water was pouring down so hard she could hardly see the Alvera house across the street. "Dumb rain! Dumb rain!" she protested.

"Yeah!" chorused her twin brothers, Juan and Ricardo. "Rain, rain, go away, come again some other day. Juan and Ricardo want to play. Inside Lolita has to stay."

They broke into laughter as she tossed a pillow at them. "Well, it's just not fair," she continued. "I want to go visit Goldie and her puppies. They're getting so big. And they're so much fun. I wish we could have one. I just love animals."

"Sí, me, too," Maria agreed. "I love our cat Dinah-mite. But I want a dog, too. Do you think Mama would let us keep one of Goldie's pups?"

Juan grinned and pointed at the rain pounding the windowpane. "If this keeps up, maybe Noah's ark will float by and bring us some pets of our own."

Just then the phone rang. It was Sam.

"Maria" she called. "Guess what? You know my mom works down at the animal shelter? Well, they're going to put on a 'Petting Circle' day. There will be a dog show and adoption clinic and experts and animal tricks and exotic animals and everything. And Aunt Caitlin and her cousin Candy say their Four-Legged Friends Pet Store will help sponsor it. Prizes and everything. They're calling it 'Ark in the Park.' And it'll be even better than their last show."

Maria laughed. "Well, if they're calling it the 'Ark,' they sure picked out a good name. I mean, it's already raining cats and dogs."

"Oh, and I've got more news, too," Sam continued. "Angie's mom's getting out of the hospital today. LaToya's sister Tina, who works there, will make sure she gets home all right. And Miss

Kitty goes back to Danville for a callback interview on a job."

Maria sighed. "All the way to Danville? Oh, Sam! If she moves there we'll never see her again. I mean, Ric Romero moved to Summer City, and now we only see him once in a while. Well, I sure hope she doesn't get the job. I mean, I know she needs a job, but — well, I still wish she'd get a new job here in Circleville. It's hard being patient and waiting for God's answer to our prayers, isn't it? Anyway, I'll call all the PTs and Zone 56 kids and see if we can put on a pet show."

"What?" Brittany cried when Maria called her. "But we're already super-busy getting ready for the big Talent Show."

"But you could bring Hope and Sweetie to the show," Maria reminded her. "There will be a play yard for all the dogs to play together unleashed."

"Oh, yes, they'd love that. Okay, count me in."

The other PTs said yes, too. A lot of planning and work was needed to get the pet show together, but everyone helped. And having the rain stop was the biggest help of all.

What a day! There was one big display of animal photos and paintings — with Angie's and Sara's folks' work winning several prizes. Angie made a poster telling

about Goldie's pups for adoption. The pups themselves were too young to come. Angie's mom was even able to come. She still had to be in a wheelchair, but she took pictures of her daughter's work to send to Angie's dad.

The kittens and cats mostly stayed in their carriers, but they did have a little enclosed play yard for them, and lots of balls of yarn. There was even a purring contest — with the winner none other than old Mrs. Greenleaf's cat Starlight. Mrs. Greenleaf was so proud — and she used to hate cats.

"See," Mrs. Greenleaf said, "Starlight has learned to be patient." Maria giggled at that. She thought Mrs. Greenleaf was the one who finally learned to be patient with Starlight.

Sara's big dog, Tank, let little children ride on his back like a pony. Juan and Ricardo brought their turtles and lizards and Petie brought his hamster. Sam and Petie and Sneezit did some special tricks together, which everyone loved. Maybe Principal Anderson would let Sneezit do them for the Talent Contest, too.

Miss Kitty — between job interviews — was there, also. "I wish I knew something definite," she sighed. "It's so hard to be patient, isn't it?"

She and Aunt Caitlin manned the hot dog booth. Pastor Andy walked around taking pictures of people with their pets for a small fee. Everyone did something to help raise money for the animal shelter. And, of course, a Circleville Sentinel reporter was on hand to let the whole world know that the "Petting Circle" was a huge success.

At last it was time to pack up and leave. The dogs were let loose in the dog park area while everyone got ready. Finally their owners whistled for them. Then the dogs all left.

All the dogs, that is, except for —

"Sneezit!" Sam called. "Where are you, boy?"

Her little dog had completely vanished!

· Good News ·
from God's Word

During a rainstorm, it's sometimes hard to be patient and wait for the sun to shine again. But what if it started raining hard, and looked as though it would never stop?

Noah's Sons' Wives Make Friends
GENESIS 6-8

I bet you love being around animals, too. Cats, birds, dogs, parakeet, goldfish — all these and more have been people's pets for thousands of years. So have monkeys and rabbits and crickets and horses and turtles and ferrets and goats.

But what would you think if someone gave

you a zebra for a pet? Or an elephant? Or a rhino or giraffe? Or even a lion or tiger or bear, oh, my! You'd probably say, "Thanks, but we don't have room in our back yard. Maybe you'd better give them to a zoo instead."

Well, the Bible tells us about some women who had all these animals for pets and more. And they didn't even have a back yard. They didn't have a front yard, either. In fact, they lived on a boat.

They were Noah's family, of course. We all hear a lot about Noah and his faith in God. We hear about how hard he and his sons worked to build the Ark. But have you ever thought about the women on the Ark — Noah's wife and daughters-in-law?

They had a big job to do, too. Besides cooking meals for the family and doing laundry (with no place to dry), they were busy feeding and caring for

all the animals. That meant bringing food and water for the chickens, ducks, rabbits, cows, horses, raccoons, mountain lions, and all the rest. Their stalls and roosting places had to be kept clean and warm. And of course all the animals needed a daily quotient of HAP — that is, Hugs And Petting. That way, they kept all the animals in the Ark HAPpy!

A Verse to Remember

"Be still before the Lord and wait patiently for him"

— **Psalm 37:7**

Where Is Sneezit?

Sneezit, Sam's little dog, has suddenly disappeared. See if you can trace his travels through this maze. Be patient — it's tricky. Then rush on to Chapter 9 to see if he's been found yet.

Puzzle answers begin on page 182.

The Winners Circle Puzzle

Add Secret Letter "P" for "patient" in space 1 of the puzzle.

Chapter 9

Two by Two

"Sneezit" everyone ran around calling. "Here, boy! Here, boy! Where are you, Sneezit?"

By now it was getting late and cool. Petie sat down, crying. "I'm too tired to look any more" he sobbed. "My backpack's getting too heavy. I want God to find Sneezit for us."

He took off his heavy backpack.

He suddenly heard a little yip. And out

jumped Sneezit—right out of Petie's backpack.

Sam and Petie stared at each other. "How in the world did he get in there?" she cried.

Petie wiped his tears. "God put him in there," he said. And that was the end of that, as far as Petie was concerned.

"Okay, the 'Petting Circle' is over," Sam announced. "Now nothing to worry about but the Talent Contest."

Sunday morning their Bible lesson was about Rebekah — and her twin babies. One day she and Isaac had no children. By the next day, they had two. Life sure changed when you had a family.

"Even though I'm an orphan," Miss Kitty said, "I'm so glad for Ma Jones. Together we're a family. Please pray that I don't have to move away from Circleville for a new job. Now I can see her at least once or twice a week at her convalescent home. If I move away, I don't know when I might be able to see her. Remember, our Bible verse to learn this week is Psalm 68:6: 'God set the lonely in families.' He did it because He loves us and never wants us to be lonely again."

The next day Mr. Talley, their social studies teacher, announced a new project for everyone: Family Circles. "Senior Circles, Petting Circles, Family Circles" teased Josh. "Now I'm really going around in circles. I'll probably even have circles under my eyes."

Mr. Talley explained the rules. Everyone was to write about their immediate family. Also, if possible, about their grandparents and any other ancestors they could find out about. "And see how they have helped make you the person you are today," he said. "How you are like them — and how you are different. Family photos can help. Interview family members. Look up your family name on the Internet. You might be surprised at what you can discover. And by the way,  five pages is the minimum to turn in for this. Your family is worth it."

Everyone set to work. Both Jenna and Maria had twins in their family. They soon discovered there had been other twins in their families in the past. Maria was already going to tell a story about her family for the Talent Contest. So her job was half done. She added copies of photos, and even one page her grandmother had written in Spanish. LaToya  wrote about one of her ancestors who'd been captured and brought to America as a slave. Sonya wrote about her Cherokee ancestors and the Trail of Tears they made from North Carolina to Oklahoma. Angie wrote about her sick mother and her father overseas, her Grandma Gretchen in Pennsylvania who raised turkeys and tulips, and how one of her ancestors fought in the Revolutionary War.

But Le was discouraged. "The only family I have left is Mom. My dad died. And both my grandparents died in Vietnam. I don't even have any aunts and uncles left that we know of. What should I do?"

Sam gave her a hug. "Pray about it," she said. "I'll pray with you. God will help you think of something."

And He did. When time came to hand in their reports on Family Circles and tell about them in class, Le told about her parents' and grandparents' life in a little village in Vietnam. She told how hard it was to lose contact with her relatives, but that God had given them all a new family here in the United States.

Her mother was now engaged to Dr. Phan, a widower. Both of them were musicians. Dr. Phan's little boys, Michael and Nicholas, would soon be her brothers. "And I have a new family at both my church and Dr. Phan's church," she added. "All those Christians are my brothers and sisters. Even Maria and LaToya. Don't we look like sisters?"

Everyone laughed at that.

LaToya grinned. "Okay, 'sis.' Then I guess it's your turn to do dishes tonight."

· Good News ·
from God's Word

Sometimes we like to daydream about what life would be like if we didn't have brothers or sisters, if we didn't have to do chores, if we didn't have to be disciplined by our parents.

Rebekah Has Twins

GENESIS 24, 25

When Isaac married Rebekah, he thought she was the most beautiful girl in the world. He had been sad since his mother died, but his father Abraham was still alive. And now he had a family of his own. All he needed for that new little family to be complete was some children.

He and Rebekah waited and waited. But no children came. They prayed and prayed. Still no children came. Rebekah had been away from her own parents now for years. She missed them very much. Then Isaac's father died. He missed him very much. Their family was now smaller than ever. Wasn't God ever going to answer their prayers?

Then one day God did answer their prayers. He gave them not just one baby, but two. Two baby boys. They named them Jacob and Esau. Some twins are alike, but these two were as different as could be. Esau loved sports. Jacob loved cooking and quiet things. But they both loved their parents. And their parents loved them both, too, for they were all one family—one family created by God.

A Verse to Remember

"God sets the lonely in families"

— Psalm 68:6

Showing My Family Love

As you think about your family and how much you love them, what can you do to show that love? Write some ideas down on the lines below. Then put a date after each idea on the day you actually do it.

How I Can Show My Love   **Date**

_____   _____

_____   _____

_____   _____

My Family Album

Inside the frames on this page and the next, draw or paste a picture of members of your family. If you want to use photos, don't paste the real photo; instead, make a copy. It only costs a few cents and keeps the photo in good shape.

The Winners Circle Puzzle

Add Secret Letter "T" for "thank God for families" to space 3 of the puzzle.

PONYTAILS FOR JESUS CHRIST

Chapter 10

What About Us Kids?

LaToya and Le were so excited when they ran into their youth group room, they couldn't even sit down.

"Whoa" laughed Pastor Andy. "What's up?"

"It's about our praise band's part in the Talent

Contest," LaToya explained. "We're now the 'Toot 'n Granny."

Pastor Andy wrinkled his nose. "You mean 'hootenannies,' don't you?"

Le giggled. "No, 'Toot 'n Granny.' See, Josh's been taking trumpet lessons, so he'll 'toot' his horn. We'll do things country-western style. Le'll play her fiddle, Brittany'll be on the ukelele, Garrett's on kettle drums — except they'll be real pots and kettles, Ric's on bass, LaToya will do guitar, Kevin's on the harmonica. And LaToya's Granny B will do the washboard and the banjo. She's the 'Granny' — get it?

"Anyone else who wants to join us can do tambourines or combs or accordions or stomp your feet or do anything else you can think of. We'll all be wearing jeans and straw hats or bonnets."

"I can play combs" Sam cried.

"But what songs are you playing?" Pastor Andy asked.

By now Josh had arrived. "Kevin and I wrote a couple of praise songs," he said. "We've been practicing them. But we want to start out with something everyone knows."

LaToya nodded. "So Maria and I wrote new words to 'On Top of Old Smoky,' 'Row, Row, Row Your Boat' and 'I've Been Working on the Railroad.' Now they're Christian songs. We want the other kids to see that we're unashamed of the Gospel, but that

Christians can have fun, too. And we'd love for all of them to come to Zone 56 and find that out for themselves."

On the way home from church that evening, Sam was already practicing the songs on her comb. "Can I be in your band, too?" Petie asked. "You big guys get all the fun, and us little kids never get any. Betcha Juan and Ricardo and me and Suzie could do something, too, if you'd help us."

Sam talked with the other PTs, and soon they decided to have yet another "circle of fun" — this time a Kids' Circle. Besides Petie and his cousin and Maria's two little brothers, they invited Jenna's little sister and Le's Mom's fiancé's two sons.

Everything was planned for outdoors. But it rained again. So they all ran down to the basement. The PTs helped the kids tell knock-knock jokes and sing and play music and games. They even had a hot dog and macaroni feast, with ice cream cups. Sneezit loved running around and barking at everyone.

Then they showed a Bible video of Sarah and Abraham and little Lot. They talked about being true to God, even when it was hard.

Afterward, the kids helped clean up.

But Sam did discover something. Jenna's little sister Katie could play the combs even better than she could. "Say, Katie" Sam said. "How would like to wear a bonnet and join the 'Toot 'n Granny'?'

Katie hugged her. "Yea!" she cheered. "Little kids can have fun like the big kids, after all."

Sam grinned. *And, oh, boy, what real fun it's going to be when our band wins First Prize in the Contest!*

· Good News · from God's Word

Some kids are embarrassed to let their friends know they love Jesus. How sad Lot would have been if Aunt Sarah and Uncle Abraham hadn't been willing to share their love — and their love for God.

Sarah and the Orphaned Lot

GENESIS 11:24-12:9

Abraham and his wife Sarah were part of a close-knit family. They lived in the big city of Ur, which today is part of Iraq. Grandfather Terah had three sons, Nahor and Haran and Abraham, who was

also called Abram. They had lots of money and good jobs.

But there were also problems. Their family loved and worshipped the one true God. But almost all of their friends and neighbors didn't. They worshipped pagan gods they could make and put in temples. Most people worshipped the moon god. They thought it was silly to worship a God they couldn't see — a Spirit who made the heavens and earth, and who had made them too. This made it hard for Abraham's family to be true to God.

Then something sad happened. Haran and his wife died. And they left a little boy, an orphan named Lot.

It happened that Abraham and his wife Sarah didn't have any children of their own. So they adopted little Lot. He became part of their family. They taught him to worship God, too.

Later God called Abraham to take all his family and leave Ur. Lot went along. First they moved to a town called Haran (like Lot's father's name). Then later they moved to Israel. Lot was always thankful for the love Sarah and Abraham gave him, and for their teaching him to worship and honor God, even when it was hard.

A Verse to Remember

*"I am not ashamed of the gospel,
because it is the power of God for the salvation of
everyone who believes"*

— Romans 1:16

Combo on the Comb

Did you know that simple little combs can make music? Take a man's pocket comb and fold a piece of wax paper over it. Put it up against your lips, with the top of the comb on top. Then hum a song. It may take a few minutes for you to discover just how close your lips should be to get the best sound. It will tickle your lips. It sounds especially good on fast, staccato (jumpy) notes.

Have Your Own Hootenanny

Here are the songs LaToya and Maria wrote for the 4J2U praise band, and the melodies to sing them with. You'll find that you can sing along, too.

"What If He Never Loved Me?"
(to the tune of "On Top of Old Smoky")

What if He never loved me?
What if He never cared?
If His heart of compassion,
He never had shared?
What if He hadn't died there
On dark Calvary?
What if He never loved me?
Oh, where would I be?

"Jesus Is the Way"
(to the tune of "Row, Row, Row Your Boat")

Jesus is the way,
The truth, the life, the King.
He's my Savior, He's my Friend,
He's my everything.

"I Was Goofing Off and Lazy"

(to the tune of "I've Been Working on the Railroad")

I was goofing off and lazy,
All the live-long day.
I was goofing off and lazy
Just to pass the time away.
Then someone told me about Jesus,
Saying, "Wake up! Don't goof your life away!
You've a Friend who loves and helps you.
Come to Him today."

Jesus, this I know,
Jesus, this I know,
Jesus is my Help and Friend.
Jesus, this I know,
Jesus, this I know,
He'll be with me to the end.

There's no Friend as true as Jesus,
There's no Friend as true, I know,
There's no Friend as true as Jesus —
That is why I love Him so!

The Winners Circle Puzzle

Add Secret Letter "U" for "unashamed of the Gospel" to space 2 of the puzzle.

Chapter 11

What Comes First?

As soon as she heard the news, Le called Sonya to tell her. "Guess what?" Le cried. "Mom and Dr. Phan have set the date. They're going to get married at Faith Church this summer. And Dr. Phan said I could start calling him 'Poppa Phan' if I want. Boy, Sonya. Life is changing so fast it makes me dizzy."

"Oh, that's wonderful, Le! Hey, let me call you back. Sam's on the other line."

"Sonya, guess what?" Sam said. "I just heard from Miss Kitty. She's going to be working for your dad. Yes, at the Superservice Automotive Headquarters in Summer City. But she'll mostly be working out of her home and will only commute to the city when they need her. So she'll be able to keep going to our church and to Whispering Pines to see Ma Jones, after all. Isn't God good?"

Sonya grinned. Wow! Yes, God was good. He was very good. Miss Kitty working for Sonya's dad? Then maybe they would start dating. And maybe Miss Kitty would be Sonya's new mother. Ever since Miss Kitty and her boyfriend Bob broke up, Miss Kitty seemed a little lonely. And Sonya's dad had been lonely ever since Sonya's mother, Mrs. Silverhorse, was killed in that accident.

God had brought someone new into Le's life.

And now she was going to have a new dad and two new brothers. Maybe God could do something wonderful like that for Sonya. Didn't the Bible say that God could do the impossible? Well, Sonya was certainly going to pray about it. And talk to her dad about it, too.

But when she did, Mr. Silverhorse just smiled.

"You want me to date a new employee? That could cause problems at work and it might make us both lose our jobs."

But Miss Kitty came to Sonya's next wheelchair basketball game. She took pictures of Sonya's playing and showed them to Sonya's dad. Yea! But Pastor Andy was there, too. And he and Miss Kitty sat together and shared a big tub of popcorn. Sonya felt so discouraged at that, she almost missed a basket. But her team won, anyway.

The other PTs were doing great, too. Everyone was doing their best to keep up their regular school work and their chores — and all their practice for the big Talent Contest. Sam finally got the costumes done for her and Petie — and Sneezit — for their special tricks act.

"The funny part about it, Maria," she explained to her friend, "is that when I was trying to get Sneezit to do tricks by himself he didn't want anything to do with it. But now that all three of us are doing it together, he's crazy about it. You wouldn't believe how fast he's learning."

Sam was also busy with Sonya making new clothes for the dolls Sam had been given. When they got together to work on them, they called it their "Sewing Circle." Angie finished her portraits of Goldie and her pups. She decided to give the pups names — Hunny, Bunny, Funny, Sunny, and Speckle Spots. Angie's mom was so proud of her, she said Angie could adopt one of the pups. Angie was thrilled, but they were all so cute — which one should she pick?

Jenna and Brittany and Sara and Maria were all doing great with their routines. In fact, Maria had added a slide show to her story about her family. And they were all having a ball practicing with their "Toot 'n Granny" praise band.

"I can't believe your Granny B is so much fun" Brittany giggled to LaToya. "And to think she does it all while she's in a wheelchair."

But with homework and chores and so much practice, they were all getting exhausted.

"Something's got to give," Sam decided.

"Si, but what?" countered Maria. "Want to stop eating and sleeping?"

"No, silly. But maybe we should give up church till the contest is over. Do you think God would mind?"

"I think you'd better ask Miss Kitty that question yourself," Maria said.

Sunday morning their Bible lesson was about Ten Wedding Guests — ten girls who'd been invited to a wedding. "They all got dressed," said Miss Kitty. "They knew the wedding would be at night and that they would need to take lamps with them. They would need oil for their lamps, too. Five of the girls brought extra oil, but the other five didn't want to bother. When the time came for the wedding parade, their lamps ran out of oil. And they ended up missing the wedding, just because they didn't have the right priorities."

"What does 'priorities' mean, Miss Kitty?" Angie asked.

"It means knowing what is important in life — what should come first. For instance, if you have a big math test coming up, which is more important: studying for it, or watching a bunch of reruns on TV? Which is more important: doing your own thing, or doing what God wants you to do? You see, God wants us to have the right priorities. He wants us to always do the right thing, even if it's a little hard. You PTs always need your RPs — your right priorities."

A little hard? It was really hard! Sam wondered, *Shouldn't my right priorities be winning this Contest for God? And if I don't practice lots, how in the world can I do it?*

· Good News · from God's Word

Sam struggled over how to figure out the right priorities in her life. So did ten girls in Jesus' day. See what happened next!

Ten Wedding Guests
MATTHEW 25:1-13

Everyone loves to go to weddings. They did back in Jesus' day, too. We love to see the beautiful, happy bride and her proud, handsome bridegroom.

Everyone else dresses up, too. Besides the wedding ceremony itself, with all the flowers and music, there's usually a big feast. Plus, of course, there are lots of cards and presents. Everyone wants to wish the new couple well.

Sometimes everyone's invited. Sometimes there's not room for everyone to attend, especially at the wedding banquet, so people get special invitations.

One day Jesus told about ten girls who'd been invited by the bridegroom to come to his wedding. The feast would be at night, though they didn't know just when. But when the bridegroom and his friends would finally show up, they'd all make a parade through the streets to the bride's house — a parade full of lights and laughter. And, of course, they wanted these girls to enjoy the party, too.

People didn't have electric lights or flashlights in those days. Instead, the girls all had oil lamps they carried. Five of the girls brought extra oil. The other five didn't bother. They'd rather just have fun.

The bridegroom and his party didn't come by until midnight. By then the lamps were all out of oil. But the wise girls just put in their backup supply of oil, re-lit their lamps, and hurried off with the crowd. The other girls rushed off in the middle of the night to try to find extra oil. By the time they found some, the wedding feast had already begun. They missed it. Why?

Just because they had the wrong priorities.

A Verse to Remember

"Seek first his kingdom and his righteousness, and all these things will be given to you as well."
— Matthew 6:33

RPs* for YOU
(*Right Priorities)

Think of all you do each day and all you do each week. That might include clubs, shopping, classes, studying, Bible reading, praying, attending church, hanging out at the mall, music practice, taking care of your clothes, chores, showers, showing love to your family, homework, and all the rest.

List them. They are probably all important. But
which do you think God wants you to consider most
important? Mark it with a check mark or star. You
should consider that most important, too.

1. _____

2. _____

3. _____

4. _____

5. _____

6. _____

7. _____

8. _____

9. _____

10. _____

The Joyful Bride

Here's a bride ready for her wedding. See how happy she is? Give her some flowers, a veil, and decorate her gown.

The Winners Circle Puzzle

Add Secret Letter "R" for "right priorities" to space 15 of the puzzle.

Chapter 12

When a Little is a Lot

Sam jumped up from the sewing machine to catch the phone. "Miss Kitty!" she cried. "Wish you were here. Sonya and I are just finishing up making outfits for all the dolls Aunt Irene gave me. They are so adorable. It's going to be so much fun putting them on exhibit for the Talent Show. And we're going to give them to needy kids afterwards."

"I do appreciate what you and Sonya are doing to help needy kids," the teacher replied. "Actually, that's what I called about. Ted McAfee, who runs the big McAfee Farms here in the county, is a good friend of Sonya's dad. He called me at work with a request.

"See, Ted's worried about the children of his farm workers. They're too shy to attend our churches here in town. He wondered if we could take church to them — that is, start Saturday morning Bible classes for them."

"Wow!" Sam cried. "That would be wonderful. But what would we use for materials?"

"Well, Faith Church has some extra study guides and videos we can borrow. So does the La Vita Spanish church. In fact, Pastor Lopez wants to come along and help. So do some of the kids there. And Maria can help, too. We can do crafts and  music and games. What we'll need most are willing hands. And prayer."

Sam put her hand over the phone as she explained the idea to Sonya. "Count me and Sonya in," she told Miss Kitty. "And I bet you can count on the other PTs too."

That Saturday morning Sam woke up to the strangest sound. The wind was howling outside. Then her phone rang. "Sam, it's Miss Kitty. Can you and Petie round up all the string and tape and long sticks and newspapers you can? I think this will be a great kite-making day for our Bible class."

When the PTs piled out of the Faith church van, the wind tugged at their clothes. Even so, about 30 children stood there in the wind waiting for them. "Miss Teacher, Miss Teacher" they called to Miss Kitty. "Bienvenidos! Welcome! When do we start?"

Miss Kitty looked around. "A better question is where do we start? I thought Mr. McAfee had a place for us to meet."

Just then Pastor Lopez drove up with his van. Out tumbled more kids. He found someone to talk to who worked on the farm. "We're to meet in the tool shed," he explained to Miss Kitty. "They have some picnic tables set up in there for us."

The problem was, the doors on the shed wouldn't close. That wind just howled right through the shed. Was it ever cold! Pastor Lopez taught them some Christian songs and Miss Kitty told a Bible story. Maria led in prayer. Then the children made kites out of newspaper and sticks. They used felt markers to write "Jesus loves you" and other messages on their kites and tied string to them. Then they all ran outside to try them out.

After a snack and hug time, it was time to go. "Thank you. Gracias" the children called. "Please come back next week."

Sam and Petie loved it. They could hardly wait for next Saturday to come. But this time when Sam woke up, it was pouring rain. "No outside games today," she sighed. "We'll have to stay in that stupid old tool shed."

As it turned out, the tool shed roof hadn't been repaired in years. The rain poured right through it. There wasn't even any electricity for lights. So that Saturday some of the children climbed into one of the vans and some climbed into the other one and they had classes in the vans. Even though they were all cramped inside, the children were full of smiles. "Please come back next week," they called.

"Of course we will," Sam promised, even though she was soaking wet too. But they couldn't keep meeting in the vans forever. What in the world could they do?

· Good News · from God's Word

Sam and her friends wanted to help these sweet children who were so needy. Likewise, long ago other girls and their poor, needy families discovered how much God loved and wanted to help them.

The First Passover
EXODUS 12, 13

Pretend you were one of the Israelite girls living in Egypt back in Moses' time. Life was hard.

All God's people were slaves. It was hard for them to worship God, because the Pharaoh, who was Egypt's king, didn't want them to. The Pharaoh thought worshipping God instead of working hard for Pharaoh was just a waste of time.

God's people had been living in Egypt for 400 years. Now, God told Moses, it was time for His people to go back to Israel. When they had first moved to Egypt, back in Jacob and Joseph's time, there were less than 100 of them. Now they numbered a million and a half. Pharaoh liked having that many slaves — people who had to obey him and work for him without pay.

"God says, 'Let My people go,'" Moses told Pharaoh.

"No way," said Pharaoh. So God sent all kinds of problems on Pharaoh and his people to change Pharaoh's mind. We call these problems "plagues." God turned the river to blood, He filled the land with frogs and stinging gnats and flies and boils and sick animals. He even sent hail and locusts. "All right, all right," Pharaoh would say, "they can go." But then he would change his mind.

Now God was ready to present His last and worst plague. He knew it would be really terrible, and the Pharaoh would tell them to leave. So He wanted His people to be ready.

"Pack up all your clothes and things and get your animals together," God said. "Don't go to bed tonight. Stay dressed and ready to leave. Roast a lamb or  goat. Call your Jewish friends in and share your meal with them. You will also serve bitter herbs.

"Take some blood from the animal and put it on the sides and top of your front door. Tonight the firstborn child of every Egyptian will die. But if the Angel of Death sees the blood on your door, he will pass over you."

The girls had to work very hard helping their mothers pack everything up and fix this meal, all the while babysitting and doing their other chores. Ever since, this very special meal has been called the Passover meal, because that is when the Angel of Death passed over the homes of believers and didn't let them get hurt.

Pharaoh did let God's people go. For the first time in their lives, these poor, needy slaves were free to live and work and worship God the way God wanted them to.

Even today Jews celebrate Passover each year. They usually celebrate for a whole week. But the Passover Meal itself is always the Thursday before Easter. Today we Christians call it the Last Supper, because when Jesus celebrated the Passover with His disciples, that was His last meal before He died on a Cross — and rose from the dead!

A Verse to Remember

"Be openhanded toward your brothers and toward the poor and needy in your land."

— ***Deuteronomy 15:11***

Go Fly a Kite

You can buy a kite kit at the store or make your own. To make your own, you'll need:
- Newspaper, wrapping paper, or lightweight paper
- Two thin dowel rods, 18-24 inches
- Twine
- Kite string
- Ribbon for the tail

Directions:
- Lay the sticks out in the shape of a T
- Wrap twine around the sticks where they cross

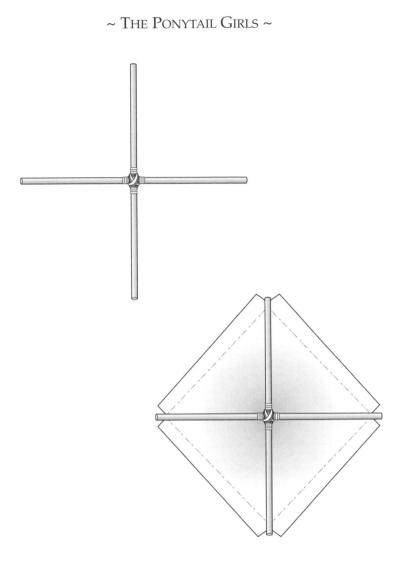

• Tie string around the sticks in a kite (diamond) shape
• Cut a diamond shape out of the paper that is two inches wider than the sticks
• Lay the sticks on the back side of the paper
• Fold the paper over the kite string frame and paste or tape in place
• Tie the long kite string to the base of the kite frame
• Add a tail at the base of the kite frame

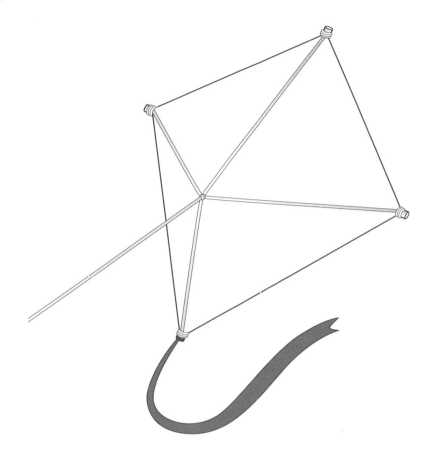

Decorate the front of the kite if you wish. This is a great project to work on with an older brother or sister or parent. Or if you use a kit from a store, you can work on it with younger brothers and sisters.

The Winners Circle Puzzle

Add the Secret Letter "S" for "seeking to help the needy" to space 10 of the puzzle.

Chapter 13

40 Days and 40 Nights

That week Miss Kitty made a lot of phone calls, including to Mr. McAfee, the farm owner. And the following Saturday several men from Faith Church and La Vita Church and Superservice Automotive showed up. They delivered a metal

building that was ready to assemble and built a
foundation for it higher than the ground around to
keep the water out, with a ramp for wheelchairs.
Then they put the building together, complete with a
sign saying "McAfee Farms Family Hall." There was
even electricity, a bottled water stand, and lots of
folding chairs and tables.

The children could hardly wait to run inside
and try it out.

And their families were so happy about the
new building that the following Saturday the
children all wrote thank you notes to Mr. McAfee and
the other men who had worked so hard. Then
everyone had a yummy enchilada feast.

The next week the farm families made curtains
for the new McAfee Farms Family Hall and hung
them up. They also put up work schedules and
calendars and pictures of their families. Someone
donated two electric heaters and someone else
donated some old baby cribs and toys. Shelves for
canned food and pots and paper plates appeared.
They even put an American flag up out front. How
proud they were of their new hall.

"We can teach English classes here now,"
someone said. "And start after-school programs for
the kids. Maybe we can have church services, too."

Just then Mother Nature also donated
something — rain. Yes, it started raining again, and
it rained and it rained and it rained. Since most of the
events the PTs had planned for the Talent Contest
were indoors, the downpour didn't stop most of their
practicing. But it did mean a lot of umbrellas, boots,

raincoats, rain-drenched ponytails, soggy backpacks, and sloshing through water-filled streets. Sonya couldn't get through the high water with her wheelchair, and had to be driven to school instead.

But as bad as it was in town, it was worse out in the countryside. Crawdad Creek was soon over its banks, covering most of the McAfee Farms fields. And then —

Le saw it on the evening news and called Jenna right away. "Jenna, did you see what happened at the McAfee Farms? The field workers' houses have been flooded out. Some of the oldest ones even washed away. And a big tree fell and crashed on two more. They're all taking refuge in that new Hall."

Soon everyone who could rushed to the Hall to help. Fortunately, since it had been built on a higher foundation, the water didn't get inside the Hall. The Salvation Army, the Red Cross, the local Emergency Response team, the Sheriff's deputies, and more showed up on the farm. Even Sara's big brother and his high school friends joined the animal rescue team, looking for missing dogs, cats, horses, and cows.

But one of the animals didn't need to be rounded up — Cocky, the rooster. His owner, Lilia Lancaster, brought him into the hall in her backpack.

Miss Kitty stared. "Is that a ch-chicken?"

"Not just any chicken," Lilia shot back. "This is Cocky. He's my bestest friend. And he's smarter'n a whip. He can dance and count to four. He's much too smart to bark or meow. And he can even drink lemonade out of a straw, so there!"

Some of the Salvation Army workers had brought electric hot plates with them, and soon workers were passing out bowls of soup. They had brought sleeping bags and cots, too. But the hall was much too small for all the farm families to stay in overnight. And there was certainly no room inside for all the animals.

"Mr. McAfee," Mrs. Pearson said, "if you can get some farm trucks and drivers together, we can get all the animals over to the Animal Shelter. We can feed them there, and they'll be safe."

"And I'll call Brother John down at the Rescue Mission," Miss Kitty added. "There should be room there for some families. Maybe our local schools could also have room for cots and sleeping bags."

Lilia held tightly to Cocky. "If they won't let Cocky stay with me, I'm not going," she said. "He's my bestest friend."

Mrs. Pearson smiled. "Then you and Cocky can come stay at my house, dear, if it's all right with your mother. We already have a dog and a cat. So Cocky should feel right at home."

Actually, Cocky did feel right at home at Sam's house. Sneezit, on the other hand, was so shocked to see the rooster he couldn't even bark. Little Sunlight, the kitten, dove headfirst under the couch and didn't come out for three days.

"Oh, dear" Sam cried. "What if Sunlight starves? Now what can I do?"

· Good News · from God's Word

The PTs tried to show God's love to the poor farm workers by making sure everyone had a safe place to stay during the flood. Here's an example from the Bible about God's people sharing His love with others.

Priscilla and Aquila's Guest

ACTS 18

Did you ever sleep in a tent? A good tent can keep out both the rain and the hot sun. People have been making tents for thousands of years. Paul's friends, Aquila and Priscilla, were husband and wife.

They were tent-makers as was Paul. In fact, they had a tent-making company in the city of Ephesus.

Sometimes they all three worked together. Tents were in great demand by shepherds and soldiers and travelers. Aquila and Priscilla loved Jesus, and they made sure their tents were well made. They also tried to help people whenever they could.

One day a young man came to Ephesus from Egypt. Apollos was his name. Apollos was a Jew who loved God's Word and looked for God's Son to come. He had been told all about John the Baptist and how the Messiah was coming. He was so happy about that, he couldn't stop telling everyone.

"The Messiah is coming!" he told all the Jews at the synagogues. "The Messiah is coming! Get ready for the Messiah!"

Apollos was a great preacher. Everyone loved to hear him. There was just one little problem. Messiah is another name for Jesus. Apollos didn't know that Jesus had already come.

So Priscilla and Aquila decided to show love to him two ways. First, they invited him to their house for a delicious, home-cooked meal. Priscilla was a great cook — just like Apollos' mother back in Egypt.

Then after dinner they sat with him and told him the wonderful story about Jesus, God's Son.

Now Apollos was more excited than ever. After that, everywhere he went, he shared the Good News about Jesus. How glad he was that Priscilla and Aquila showed God's love to him by their kindness.

A Verse to Remember

"Let us do good to all people"

— Galatians 6:10

Cocky the Rooster

Here's a picture of Lilia's pet rooster, Cocky, to color. If you wish, you can show him drinking lemonade with a straw from a cup.

The Winners Circle Puzzle

Add Secret Letter "T" for "trying to show God's love" to space 4 of the puzzle.

Chapter 14

It's Almost Time!

Sam stared at the calendar on the fridge door. "Oh, Petie" she cried. "It's almost time. And we have so much practice to do before the Talent Contest."

The last few days had been a big blur, so much was going on. When the big rainstorm finally stopped, the few cabins left on the farm were ruined. So the local station Channel 7 started a telethon. They raised enough money to replace all the cabins with mobile homes—with half of the money coming from McAfee Farms and Superservice Auto.

Soon everyone was back to the farm in their new homes. But now it was almost time for the big Contest.

Petie and Sneezit were curled up on the couch watching TV. "What do you mean?" he cried. "You and me and Sneezit already practiced our heads off. He's too tired to even wag his tail."

"Well, we have to practice even more. We want to be in the Winners' Circle, don't we?"

He shrugged. "I dunno. I just want to have fun. And it's not much fun any more. Even my Gameboy batteries are so tired they stopped working."

"Well, it will be fun when you win, I promise. Tell you what. Slip on your jacket and let's walk down to the drug store. I'll pick you up some new batteries there. They might even have some new Gameboy games for you. I've saved up $10 if you want it. What do you say?"

A short while later Petie was a happy camper 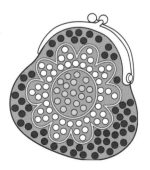 with new batteries and a new game. And Sam's wallet was empty again, but she was happy too. Anything to make it through to the Contest.

Just then she stopped and stared. Next door to the drug store was a brand-new place called Viva! And its front window was full of gorgeous dresses. "Look, Petie" Sam cried. "That red

satin one. That would be
perfect for me for the
Contest. And all it costs
is $23. Oh, I've just got
to have it!"

Petie looked up,
annoyed. "What do you
mean? You just made us
costumes for our
Magicteers Tricks Show. And you're going to wear
jeans and a straw hat for the band act. What do you
need a new dress for?"

She rolled her eyes. "For all the rest of the
night, of course — like when Sonya and I are showing
off our Doll Fashion Show. Wait'll I tell Mom about
this."

Unfortunately, Mrs. Pearson agreed with Petie.
"Good heavens, dear. You can't spend all night in the
bathroom changing costumes. Besides, you just spent
all your money."

"But, Mom, can't you lend me some? It's only
$23 dollars. I'll pay you back when I get some money.
Honest."

"That's plus tax. And that's $23 I don't have
right now, Sam. We shot our budget the last couple of
weeks on food for those poor farm workers and their
animals, remember? That's a lot more important than
a new dress. Now, better get to your homework."

But all Sam could think about was that
gorgeous red satin dress. She could wear little red
earrings with it and a red ribbon around her ponytail.

Perfect. But where could she come up with that much money? She'd just have to find it somehow.

So Sam began making phone calls. "Yes," Aunt Caitlin said, "I'd be glad to have you babysit for $10." Mr. Talley agreed to pay her $7.50 to wash his car. The Four-Legged Friends Pet Store said yes. They needed someone to clean out all the cages and put in fresh straw for $15. It was more than enough.

Unfortunately, they all wanted her to do the jobs that Saturday. So Sam made an excuse to Miss Kitty not to go to the Saturday morning Bible class out at the farm. She even coughed and cleared her voice to make it sound as if she were sick. Then after she hung up the phone, she threw on her clothes and got to work.

It took her all day long, and the sun was setting when she got home Saturday night. But there was a smile on her face and lots of bills in her wallet. Just wait till she had a chance to run back down to that Viva! store. In fact, she already had a place in her closet to hang her gorgeous new red dress.

Sunday morning in Bible class Sam had a hard time keeping her mind on the lesson about some hardworking women. Boy, if anyone was hardworking, it was Sam. Look at all she did yesterday. God must be pretty proud of her.

"But God doesn't want us just to work hard," Miss Kitty continued. "He wants us to work hard for the right reasons. And with the right attitude. He wants us to use our strength to honor Him and to help others."

Sam squirmed a little at that. "By the way," their teacher said, "please pray for me this afternoon. I'm going to take Lilia Lancaster's little sister to the doctor. She's very sick, and they don't have money for the doctor. They don't have money for food, either. With all the rain, the farm workers haven't been able to work, so they haven't been paid.

"Lilia's mom wants her to either sell Cocky or to cook him for food so they have something to eat. Lilia is heartbroken. She loves Cocky, but she loves her family, too. She doesn't know what to do. What do you think she should do, Sam?"

· Good News · from God's Word

Who should Sam put first — herself or others? Many women back in the Bible days had to make that same choice. Which do you think they chose?

Hardworking Women
— ROMANS 16

Sometimes when we think about the early Christians, we only think of men. When we think of Jesus' disciples, we sometimes forget that He had women disciples following Him, too.

The same was true of the early Church after Jesus arose from the dead. In the book Paul wrote to the church in Rome, he mentions some of them. First,

he names Phoebe—a woman who made the long, dangerous trip by boat from Greece to Italy to deliver this letter. Remember, there weren't any airplanes or the U.S. Postal Services in those days. All letters had to be delivered by hand by someone.

Then he mentions Priscilla — the tentmaker we studied last chapter. Paul says she not only worked hard all day making tents, but she and her husband had a church meet right in their own home. Remember, the Romans didn't like Christians. They kept them poor. It took many years before Christians were allowed to build churches.

Paul also mentions someone named Mary — not Jesus' mother, but someone else "who worked very hard for you." She didn't get paid for it, but she served with gladness.

He then mentions three other women who "worked very hard in the Lord." And also Rufus' mother, "who has been a mother to me, too." Paul traveled all over the world, facing shipwrecks, persecution, assassination attempts, and more. His own mother was probably dead. How he appreciated this kind woman who tried to be a "mother" to him. Then he mentions Julia and another woman.

All of them loved Jesus. And all of them worked hard to share His Gospel with others, just as God wants us to do.

A Verse to Remember

"Love your neighbor as yourself."

— **Romans 13:9**

Making Hard Choices

Sam had a hard choice to make: to buy herself a new dress, or to help out a poor sick girl. Have you

ever had a hard choice to make? Maybe you're having to make one right now! On the next page, write down what the problem is or was, and how you solved it — or how you're going to ask God to help you solve it.

_____

_____

_____

Selfless Choices

See which words from the right side are the right ones for the rhymes on the left.

1. If we really care,
   We'll always try to _____
A. You

2. The way that I should be
   Is love my neighbor as much as _____
B. down

3. You can spell JOY, it's true,
   As Jesus, Others, then _____
C. share

4. With cookies or with cake,
   The biggest piece don't _____
D. way

5. Don't brag on yourself, but try
   To brag on the other _____
E. me

6. Don't sneer at folks or frown
   Or put somebody _____
F. guy

7. Instead, smile, rejoice, and pray,
   'Cause that's the Jesus _____
G. take

Puzzle answers begin on page 182.

The Winners Circle Puzzle

Put Secret Letter "S" for "selfless" in space 12 of the puzzle.

Chapter 15

Talking in Circles

After church that day Sam's wallet was all empty again. But her heart was full. That gorgeous red dress still hung on the store rack. But Lilia's little sister got to go to the doctor. Cocky was saved! Now on to the big Contest.

The Contest was the big subject over at LaToya's house, too. "I'm so glad you're helping out our praise band, Granny B," LaToya said, as she and her grandmother did the dinner dishes together. "I love how you can do it all from your wheelchair. Sonya says you're a real inspiration to her."

Her grandmother chuckled. "You PTs are all real inspirations to me, child. How're all the practices coming for the big day?"

"Fantastic. You know the band is doing great because you practice with us. And our gymnastic team won three meets in a row."

Granny B handed back a plate. "Here, honey, you missed a spot. What about Sam and her puppy?"

LaToya giggled. "Oh, Granny B, you wouldn't believe what that little dog can do. And Sonya and Sam made new clothes for the dolls her Aunt Irene gave her. She's going to put on a Doll Fashion Show. One is a princess outfit. But the one I like best is all in pink polka dots. It even has matching pink shoes and a hat."

"What about Sonya's basketball team?"

"They won three out of the last five games, all from their wheelchairs. And, oh, you should see Jenna in her ballet scene. She looks just like a movie star. Brittany's working on her monologue, plus helping out the cheerleaders. And Le's playing both classical violin and fiddle pieces. Everyone's so busy, I get worn out just thinking about it."

Granny B wiped the last of the plates. "Didn't you say something about that new girl Angie drawing something? How's that working out?"

"Oh, Granny. First she drew all the puppies. And then Sara's folks showed her how to make paintings of them. And now she's working on cartoons of all the animals — including Cocky, the rooster. I mean, real cartoons, like you see in the funny papers. And here I can't even draw a straight line."

Granny B laughed. "Well, you can sure talk one, gal. My head's going around in circles just listening to you. Whew! I'll sure be glad when this contest is over. Speaking of circles, when I was your age our church had singing circles and prayer circles. Reading circles, too."

LaToya thought a moment. "And we PTs have had a Senior Circle, a Petting Circle, a Kids' Circle, and Sonya and Sam's Sewing Circle." She laughed. "And of course I'd like to be in the Winners Circle."

Sunday evening at Zone 56 there was a new member — Lilia Lancaster.

"Pastor Andy brought me," she said shyly. "I wanted to thank everyone for helping my little sister get better. I don't know if I really belong here, but I thought I'd try."

When she heard the praise band she became very excited. "Cocky and I do music, too," she said. "I got my grandma's old ukulele, and he can really keep time to the music. He even yells A-HA!"

Everyone looked at each other. "Can he do country-western style?" Josh asked. "If so, he's in. As long as he doesn't get too 'cocky'!"

Pastor Andy taught the Bible story of Peter's wife's mother, and how all Christians need to be sold out for God. Then they put the chairs in a circle for a game of Musical Chairs, and afterwards they prayed in a circle for each other. They also prayed for everyone competing in the big Talent Contest — yes, not just their Zone 56 friends, but everyone.

"Pastor Andy," Lilia said afterward. "What does it mean to be 'sold out for God'? Does it mean loving Him and being kind like you people are? And can I be 'sold out for God' too?"

Sam held her breath. What would Pastor Andy say?

· Good News · from God's Word

"Sold out for God" means always trying to do your best for Him. Here's a Bible story about a woman who was never famous or rich, but she always gave her best anyway.

Peter's Wife's Story

LUKE 4:38, 39

We don't know if Peter and his wife had children, but she had a busy life anyway. He was a fisherman. He needed clean clothes and help cooking all those fish. Also, Peter and his friends spent a lot of time traveling around with Jesus. When they came to her and Peter's town, they of course wanted to welcome Jesus and His other disciples. And that meant even more cooking. So then she needed her mother to help with all the work.

But one time when Jesus and His friends came, there was sad news. His wife's mother was sick. She had a high fever and nothing they could do could help her.

"Please, Jesus!" Peter and his wife cried, "Can you help her get well?"

Of course He could. And He did. And just like that she was cured. In fact, she felt so well, she jumped up out of bed, rushed to the kitchen, and began serving everyone the way she always did.

How glad Peter's wife's mother was to be able to serve again!

And how glad Peter and his wife were to have their family well again.

 # A Verse to Remember

"Stand firm in the Lord"

— *Philippians 4:1*

A Circle of Life

Here's a good thing to talk to your friends about when you're "talking in circles." It's a very familiar Bible verse. The first letter and every third letter is given. See if you can fill in the blanks. If you don't remember it all, look up John 3:16.

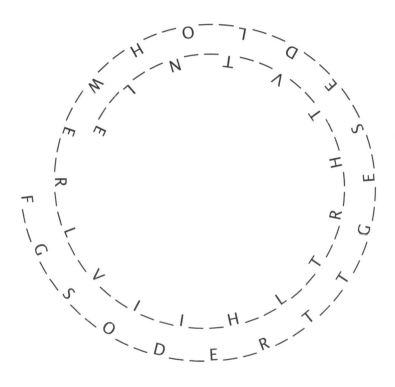

The Winners Circle Puzzle

Add Secret Letter "S" for "sold out for God" to space 16 of the puzzle.

Chapter 16

The Big Day

Sam was so shocked she could hardly breathe. Was she hearing right?

"Pastor Andy," Lilia was saying, "What does it mean to be 'sold out for God'? Can I be God's, too?"

So while the other Zone 56 kids gathered around, praying silently, Pastor Andy explained to Lilia what it meant to be a Christian. He told her all about God sending His Son Jesus to die for us on the Cross, and then rising from the dead that first Easter and being in Heaven right now to help us. He told her she needed to tell God she was sorry for all the things she'd done wrong, and ask Jesus to be her Savior. Then she would be born again. God's Holy Spirit would live in her heart. And she would be God's child to love and serve Him forever.

"Wow!" Lilia exclaimed. "So that's what the Bible's all about. I always wondered, but no one ever told me. Well, I want to be a real Christian too, Pastor Andy. I want to tell God all about it — right now! And then I'm going to tell all the kids on the farm. I'm even going to tell Cocky. Boy, I'm so glad I came today!"

Lilia attended the other Middle School in Circleville called Sunset. She hadn't thought about entering the Winners Circle Talent Contest before. But now with the other kid's encouragement, she couldn't wait to get out her grandmother's old ukulele and

join the praise band. The next day after school LaToya and Granny B drove over to the farm to teach Lilia the songs the band would be performing. Lilia's mom was so glad to show off her new mobile home.

"Look — it has bathrooms and closets and everything!" she cried. "No more leaky roofs or mold in the walls. No more falling through the broken floor. No more sick baby. Praise the Lord!"

Granny B had brought her washboard and banjo. LaToya brought her guitar. Lilia got out her ukulele and soon they were all practicing away. Suddenly someone walked in — someone uninvited — and joined them. Cocky! He fell in love with the washboard and started playing it right along with Granny B. In fact, she had to be careful not to get scratched by his claws.

Lilia hugged her pet. "Oh, Cocky. You're the greatest. I bet our band will win first prize!"

Come Root for Our School!

Soon the big day had arrived. The newspapers and TV were full of the news about the Talent Contest. There were posters all over Madison's halls. "Come root for our school!" the posters said. And then it listed some of the Madison Middle School entries in the city-wide contest.

All those registered for the Contest went over to City Hall early to get acquainted with the sound system and dressing rooms, and also to set up any exhibits. Maria set up her science exhibit, "What Cats Mean When They Talk." Sonya and Sam set up their

Doll Fashion Show. Sara's big brother Tony and his pals on the swim team filled a table on "Safety When Swimming." Angie set up a display of all her animal pictures and cartoons. Other students from other schools had book tables and travel photos and even science experiments.

And of course there were the refreshment tables to help raise money for the schools. Angie baked some chocolate chip cookies, while Granny B had a large platter of her Chocky Chunky Chewies. Maria's and Jenna's moms sold mouth-watering enchiladas. Other parent volunteers manned the coffee and lemonade stands.

So many people turned up they could hardly find a place to park. Everyone clapped for the Mayor and Town Council when they entered. The ushers invited everyone to visit all the booths and table exhibits. Then the Contest began.

"Oh, my goodness" Lilia cried. "I've never been before such a large crowd before. What if I'd too scared to play?"

Sam hugged her. "You'll be fine. God will help you not to be afraid."

Someone had set up a PowerPoint program so the names of the

contestants would appear on a big screen. Then, for variety, they alternated between live performances and videotaped ones. That way Sonya's wheelchair basketball games, LaToya's gymnastic meets, and Sara's ice skating events could all be shown on the screen. Maria also used the screen for a slide show when she talked about her family.

Brittany's cheerleading team and Jenna's dancing team performed right on stage. So did Sara's big brother Tony, who did a great juggling act. Le's violin solo was wonderful.

But Sam and Petie and Sneezit — "The Magnificant Magicteers" — brought the house down. Every time people clapped, Sneezit would stand on his hind legs and whirl around in circles — not easy for a little "wiener" dog. "Nothing can beat this" Sam whispered to Petie.

But just then Cocky strutted out on stage. Sneezit took one look at the big rooster and ran wailing off the stage — and right out into the audience.

"Sneezit!" Petie screamed. "Come back!"

· Good News · from God's Word

Sneezit was scared by a rooster. We can get scared of something new, too, can't we? Today's story is about some children who met Someone new — Jesus!

Little Children Meet Jesus

MARK 10:13-16

"Mommy! Mommy!" cried the little children. "Where are we going? Why are you walking so fast?"

"We're going to see Jesus," explained their mothers. "Jesus is God's Son. He loves little children. He can make sick children well, too. He's a very kind Man. We want Him to bless you and to pray for you."

"But, Mommy," protested one little boy, "if He's God's Son, the Messiah, isn't that scary? He's so big and powerful, aren't you afraid?"

His mother hugged him. "No, we should never be afraid of Jesus. He loves us and wants to help us."

Soon the field was full of eager mothers and children, all with smiling faces, hurrying over to where Jesus sat talking.

"Is this the line to stand in to get blessed by Jesus?" a mother asked one of Jesus' disciples.

"What?" cried the man. "Don't you know how important Jesus is? His time is much too important to waste on mere children. He's preaching about the Kingdom of God to grownups. Now, go away. Shoo."

155

How sad the mothers and children were then. They were afraid of this man.

But Jesus heard what was going on. "Stop!" He ordered. "I'm never too busy to take time to hug and bless a little child. You grownups should be as trusting and loving as these little ones are. You must be that trusting and loving if you want to be part of My Kingdom."

Then He took as many children in His arms at one time as He could and blessed them all. The children were happy. Their mothers were happy. And Jesus was happy, too.

A Verse to Remember

"Surely God is my salvation; I will trust and not be afraid"

— *Isaiah 12:2*

Granny B's Chocky Chunky Chewies

Here's the recipe to make a dessert like Granny B did for the contest.

Ingredients:
unsalted crackers
1 cup margarine or butter
1 cup semi-sweet chocolate chips
1 cup sugar
1 cup finely chopped nuts
(any kind)

Instructions:
This recipe requires an adult's help. Preheat the oven to 400 degrees Fahrenheit. Cover cookie sheet with foil. Line the foil with unsalted crackers. Melt the margarine; add sugar. Bring to boil, stirring constantly for two minutes. Pour the margarine-sugar syrup over the crackers. Bake for six minutes. Pour the chocolate chips evenly over the crackers and sprinkle with nuts. Put in freezer for 15 minutes, and then break apart.

The Winners Circle Puzzle

Put Secret Letter "U" for "unafraid" in space 11 of the puzzle. There's just one more missing letter to fill in. Have you figured out the puzzle yet?

Chapter 17

And the Winner Is…

Everyone started laughing and clapping. Soon Sneezit began to think he was missing out on something. Hey, they were clapping for that stupid rooster. Well, he was a whole lot better than any dumb chicken.

So he ran back up on stage and did his dance-on-his-hind-legs trick again in time to the music. After their country-western songs, the "Toot 'n Granny" band performed a couple of praise songs about Jesus. People really listened, too.

The PTs and their friends were only part of a long, long program, with most of the performers in high school and much older than them. One girl sang opera. A boy and girl did a scene from Romeo and Juliet, complete with costumes. There were several school band entries and some dramatic videos — kids hiking up "Monster Mountain," water skiing in Florida, and judging a horse show. Finally, all the acts were over and the judges retired to deliberate their decisions while a weary audience snacked on the last of the cookies and enchiladas.

After a while the judges returned. "Well, folks," the mayor began, "we have good news and bad news. The good news is that this has been the best Talent Contest here in Circleville for years. Our biggest crowd-pleaser tonight is obviously the country band from Madison Middle School. We forecast that they'll really go places if they try for Nashville. Let's give a big hand for the Toot 'n Granny."

Everyone clapped. Sam grinned. Yea! They won!

"However," the Mayor continued, "a quick
search of our City Council rules tonight revealed that
the only animals allowed here in City Hall are seeing-
eye dogs. I'm sorry this wasn't brought to your
principals' attention before, but we must obey the
law. So, since the 4J2U band had two animals in its
presentation, it must be eliminated from competition.
Therefore, our winners are — "

Sam's head spun. What? They were best of all
— but eliminated for a technicality? It wasn't fair. It
just wasn't fair!

She hardly heard the rest of the awards, she
was so upset. The opera singer got first place for
performing. Sara's ice skating got third place in the
videos. Angie's drawings and paintings won second
place in exhibits.

That's all? That's all? Sam stormed. But, God,
why didn't you let the PTs win more? We were great.
Think what a great testimony it would have been.
Now we're losers. She almost burst into tears.

Suddenly, she and the rest of the praise band
were surrounded by admirers and reporters. So many
people took flash pictures of Cocky he thought the
sun had come up, and started crowing.

"Your band absolutely has to do a CD or
DVD" someone suggested. "What a great way to tell
about Jesus!"

Then suddenly Sam relaxed. They hadn't
prayed to win. They'd prayed to witness to their
friends and neighbors in Circleville. And that was
just what God let them do.

Suddenly a policewoman tapped Angie's mom on the shoulder. "Mrs. Andrews," she said, "can I see you outside? You're wanted for a very important phone call. From overseas!

The PTs looked at each other. Oh, no! Was Angie's dad okay?

Right after that, the Mayor came back onstage. "Excuse me, folks, may I please have your attention again? I have a very important announcement to make."

· Good News · from God's Word

No, Sam didn't win First Place, but she won something even better — a chance to tell people about Jesus. Here's someone else who won something better than fame or riches — a chance to be free.

Miriam's Joy in Being Set Free
EXODUS 14, 15

Miriam was Moses' sister. She had been a slave her whole life. Moses had it easier. His big sister Miriam helped a Princess adopt her baby brother when he was little. So he grew up as a Prince. But one thing both of them wanted: they wanted God's people to be free again. They wanted to go back to Israel. They wanted God's people to have their own country and not be slaves in another country.

Finally they were both old people, in their eighties —
so old they almost lost hope. Then one day God
called Moses to lead the Israelites out of Egypt to
freedom. At the time, Moses was living far away, but
he obeyed God and came back to Egypt. God helped
him and his brother Aaron talk to Pharaoh, the
Egyptian king. They told Pharaoh that God said to
"let My people go."

Of course Pharaoh disobeyed God's message.
But then God sent a lot of troubles—called plagues —
on Egypt. Finally Pharaoh had enough. He told
God's people to go.

That was in the middle of the night. Everyone
was all packed up and ready to go. They set out and
headed east toward the Red Sea. God's presence led
them through the darkness with a large, tall pillar of
cloud by day and a pillar of fire by night.

Then Pharaoh changed his mind and sent his army after his slaves to bring them back. Instead, God opened up the water of the Red Sea and the people walked across it on dry land.

"Ah, ha!" cried Pharaoh. "After them!" But once all the Israelites and all their animals made it across, all the water came back with a huge crash. The Egyptian army drowned.

How thankful God's people were for His help. Especially Miriam. She and Moses wrote a song to thank God for what He had done. They taught it to the people and they all sang together. Miriam led some other women to play tambourines and dance around as they sang.

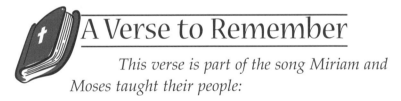

How glad she was for all God had done for them.

A Verse to Remember

This verse is part of the song Miriam and Moses taught their people:

"The Lord is my strength and my song;
He has become my salvation.
He is my God, and I will praise him."

— Exodus 15:2

Sneezit the Star

Here is Sneezit performing at part of the "Magnificent Magicteers." You can add a top hat and bow tie and cane if you wish.

The Winners Circle Puzzle

If you haven't already done so, put Secret Letter "J" for "joying in God's goodness" to space 8 of the puzzle. The puzzle is now finished. That was the easy part.

The hard part is doing what it says:

"Putting Jesus First."

Chapter 18

What's Next?

Sam stared. One minute she thought the ceremonies were over. The next, Angie's mom was being hustled out of the auditorium by a policewoman. And the Mayor was running back onstage. What in the world had happened?

"Excuse me, folks," the Mayor said. "I have a very important announcement to make. We have two special winners to add to tonight's Winners Circle.

You see, the City Council has decided to give a special Humanitarian Award to Superservice Auto and McAfee Farms for their help in improving the lives of our local farm workers. Mr. McAfee and Mr. Silverhorse, can you accept that award on behalf of all your wonderful volunteers?"

After the clapping stopped, the Mayor continued, "We also have a special award for the 4J2U 'Toot 'n Granny' Band. They weren't eligible, of course, for a regular award because their presentation included animals. But they are eligible for our brand-new Peace Prize — for promoting peace between our city's roosters and dogs." Everyone, of course, laughed at that. "And between kids and grandmothers. Granny B, could you accept that award on behalf on your band?"

As the people started to leave, Angie and her mother returned. "It was my dad" Angie cried. "We just got a call from my dad! When he couldn't reach us at home, he called the police and asked them to reach us here." She grabbed Sam's arm. "Oh, Sam! Sam! He's coming home! He's coming home!"

Afterwards, all the PTs ended up at LaToya's home for cake and ice cream, along with their families. Mrs. Alvera came over from across the street.

Mrs. Tran and Dr. Phan stood holding hands. They smiled at each other, then announced, "We want to celebrate another Winners Circle tonight. All you PT girls are invited to be bridesmaids at our wedding this summer."

The girls all squealed at that. Then Miss Kitty and Pastor Andy looked at each other and smiled, too. "We have an announcement to make, too" Miss Kitty said.

Sonya gasped. Oh, no! Surely they weren't going to get married, too?

Pastor Andy smiled. "We're going to Peru for two weeks with a group of Christian college kids — students at the college over in Summer City. We'll be helping the people in a village down there build a church. Please pray for us."

Sonya let out her breath. Whew! Then Sonya said, "Well, I have an announcement to make, too. My Cherokee friend Red Wing and her mom are coming to our house next week to visit. I'm so excited."

"Now it's my turn," added Mrs. Alvera. "Goldie's puppies are now ready to be adopted. You all have first dibs. Anyone interested?"

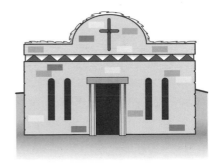

Of course! Soon Le, Angie, Lilia, LaToya, and Maria had all been promised pups.

Finally, Lilia giggled, "And I have an announcement, too. It's way past Cocky's bedtime. Pastor Andy, could you drive me and Cocky back to the farm?"

At that, everyone laughed and got ready to leave. "That reminds me," Sam said, "where's Sneezit?"

Granny B laughed. "I bet he's hiding again."

And so he was — behind the couch, sound asleep, curled up with LaToya's kitten Twilight.

LaToya laughed. "Look, they make a perfect circle curled up there, too. Another Winners Circle. Isn't God good?"

· Good New · from God's Word

Yes, God is indeed good! That's something Sarah and Abraham discovered too, when God finally gave them a baby — even though they were old enough to be grandparents.

Sarah's Joy at God's Gift
GENESIS 17, 18, 21

Sarah longed for a baby of her own. Yes, she took care of little Lot. But that wasn't the same. She loved Lot, but still she wanted a baby of her own. And she prayed for a baby, over and over again. So did her husband Abraham.

"Don't worry," God said, "you're going to have a baby."

"Yes, God, but when?" Abraham was worried. Years went by, then more and more years. Abraham's hair and beard turned gray. Sarah's hair turned gray, too. All her friends were grandmothers by now. Yet she still didn't have a baby.

Finally Sarah was almost 90 years old. Abraham was almost 100. They were far too old now to have a baby. At least they thought so. God didn't think so. In fact, He sent some angels to tell Abraham and Sarah that they would have a baby in just a year.

Sarah giggled and giggled at that. Part of her giggling was because she was so happy. But part was because she thought God was making a joke. "Everyone knows I'm way too old to have a baby now," she told herself.

But God didn't know that. And guess what? The very next year He did give Sarah the baby she had longed for for years. How thrilled Sarah was with baby Isaac!

How grateful she was to God for answering her prayers.

A Verse to Remember

"Rejoice in the Lord always. I will say it again: Rejoice!"

— **Philippians 4:4**

A Cuddly Winner's Circle

See Sneezit cuddled up asleep? But he's not alone. See if you can connect the dots to draw the kitten curled up beside him.

Extra Stuff

The following pages contain bonus Ponytail Girls activities and information especially for you. In this section you will find information on forming your own Ponytail Girls Club, including membership cards.

Another Song for You

If you enjoyed singing the country-western style Christian songs the 4J2U wrote for the big Talent Contest (see Chapter 10), here's an extra song for you to enjoy. You can sing it all in the same key, or go up half a step for each verse. Not only is this a fun song for you and your friends to sing, it's about the most wonderful event that will happen in the future — Christ's return to earth for all of us! The "He" of the song refers to Jesus.

He'll Be Comin' in Clouds of Glory

(tune: She'll Be Comin' 'Round the Mountain)

He'll be comin' in clouds of glory when He comes.
Amen!
He'll be comin' in clouds of glory when He comes.
Amen!
He'll be comin' in clouds of glory
While we sing the Old, Old Story,
He'll be comin' in clouds of glory when He comes.
Amen!

We will all rise up to meet Him when He comes.
Amen!
We will all rise up to meet Him when He comes.
Amen!
We will all rise up to meet Him
As we honor, praise, and greet Him

We will all rise up to meet Him when He comes.
Amen!

All the world will bow before Him when He comes.
Amen!
All the world will bow before Him when He comes.
Amen!
All the world will bow before Him,
They will worship and adore Him,
All the world will bow before Him when He comes.
Amen!

He'll have mansions up there for us when He comes.
Amen!
He'll have mansions up there for us when He comes.
Amen!
He'll have mansions up there for us.
We'll sing the Halleluia Chorus!
He'll have mansions up there for us when He comes.
Amen!

We will be with Him forever when He comes. Amen!
We will be with Him forever when He comes. Amen!
We will be with Him forever.
Will Jesus leave us? Never!
We will be with Him forever when He comes.
AMEN!

The Ponytail Girls Club

Would you like to be a part of a Ponytail Girls Club? You can be a PT yourself, of course. But it's much more fun if one of your friends joins with you. Or even five or six of them. There is no cost. You can read the Ponytail Girls stories together, do the puzzles and other activities, study the Bible stories, and learn the Bible verses.

Ponytail.Girls.Club Member

If your friends buy their own Ponytail Girls books, you can all write in yours at the same time. Arrange a regular meeting time and place, and plan to do special things together, just like the PTs do in the stories, such as shopping, Bible study, homework, or helping others.

Trace or copy the membership cards on page 177 and give one to each PT in your group.

Membership Cards

Trace or photocopy these cards. Fill them out, color them in and give one to each member of your Ponytail Girls club. Be sure to put your membership card in your wallet or another special place for safekeeping.

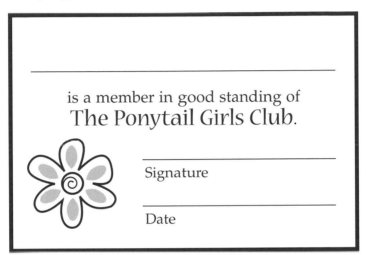

_____

is a member in good standing of
The Ponytail Girls Club.

_____
Signature

_____
Date

_____

is a member in good standing of
The Ponytail Girls Club.

_____
Signature

_____
Date

Bible Verses to Remember and Share

These are the Bible verses the PTs studied throughout this book. Copy them onto pretty paper and learn them. Share your favorites with someone else!

The Lord is my strength and my song;
He has become my salvation.
He is my God, and I will praise him.
*— **Exodus 15:2***

Be openhanded toward your brothers
and toward the poor and needy in your land.
*~**Deuteronomy 15:11***

God has the power to help.
*~**2 Chronicles 25:8***

Be still before the Lord and wait patiently for him.
*~**Psalm 37:7***

God sets the lonely in families.
*~**Psalm 68:6***

A friend loves at all times.
*~**Proverbs 17:17***

Do not forsake your friend.
*~**Proverbs 27:10***

She … works with eager hands.
*~**Proverbs 31:13***

She opens her arms to the poor
and extends her hands to the needy.
~Proverbs 31:20

Surely God is my salvation; I will trust and
not be afraid.
~Isaiah 12:2

Obey the Lord your God.
~Jeremiah 26:13

Seek first his kingdom and his righteousness,
and all these things will be given to you as well.
~Matthew 6:33

I am not ashamed of the gospel,
because it is the power of God for the salvation of
everyone who believes.
~Romans 1:16

Love your neighbor as yourself.
~Romans 13:9

Let us do good to all people.
~Galatians 6:10

Each of you should look not only to your own
interests, but also to the interests of others.
~Philippians 2:4

Stand firm in the Lord.

~Philippians 4:1

Rejoice in the Lord always. I will say it again: Rejoice!

~Philippians 4:4

Glossary (glos/ə rē)

Apollos: *ah-paul-us*
Aquila: *ah-kwill-uh*
Asphalt: *az-fault*
Bienvenidos: *bee-in-vuh-NEE-doze*
Buenos días: *bway-nos DEE-us*
Enchilada: *en-shuh-LAH-duh*
Ephesus: *eh-fuh-sus*
Esau: *ee-saw*
Fiancé: *fee-on-say*
Goliath: *go-lie-uth*
Gracias: *grah-see-us*
Haman: *hay-mun*
Haran: *hah-rahn*
Ingenious: *in-jean-yus*
La Vita: *lah vee-tah*
Michal: *my-cal*
Moab: *mow-ab*
Monologue: *mahn-oh-log*
Mordecai: *more-duh-ki*
Nahor: *nay-hore*
Pharaoh: *fay-row*
Plague: *plag*
Priorities: *pry-or-ih-tees*
Purim: *pure-eem*
Résumé: *reh-zoo-may*
Routines: *roo-teens*
Sí: *see*
Sodom: *saw-dumb*
Tabor: *tay-bore*
Terah: *tee-rah*
Viva: *vee-vuh*
Xerxes: *zerk-zeez*

Answers to Puzzles

Chapter 1

PUTTING
1 2 3 4 5 6 7
JESUS
8 9 10 11 12
FIRST
13 14 15 16 17

Chapter 2
Being the Best They Could Be, p. 35
1-Miriam, 2-Esther, 3-Dorcas, 4-Mary, 5-Lydia,
6-Rhoda, 7-Deborah

Chapter 3
PT on the QT, p. 44
1-H, 2-G, 3-I, 4-K, 5-J, 6-L, 7-B, 8-A, 9-D, 10-E, 11-M,
12-F, 13-C

Chapter 4
Word Search Puzzle, p. 54

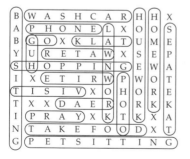

Chapter 5
Her Name in Lights, p. 61

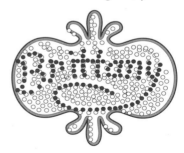